She narrowed h
what would coo
announced that
that he and this Gary were secretly
engaged. That'd make Hartsell look
like a nasty piece of work, outing
Sam like that and making him look
all sleazy, when they were keeping
it quiet so as not to detract from
the campaign." She gave Curtis
an evil grin. "Yeah, they'd look
all wholesome—a sweet, cute gay
couple heading for marriage, and
there's him, trying to make the
whole situation seem sordid."

There was a stunned silence.

Sam was the first to react. "This is *not* the plot from
a *Will & Grace* episode, all right?" His head was still
reeling from her suggestion.

"Wait a minute, wait a minute!" Josh straightened in
his chair, his eyes shining. "You might have something
there."

Two heads swiveled in his direction, and from three
mouths came the same word simultaneously: "What?"

Josh was nodding, his cheeks flushed. "This might
work to our advantage."

WELCOME TO

⌬REAMSPUN DESIRES

Dear Reader,

Love is the dream. It dazzles us, makes us stronger, and brings us to our knees. Dreamspun Desires tell stories of love featuring your favorite heartwarming heroes, captivating plots, and exotic locations. Stories that make your breath catch and your imagination soar.

In the pages of these wonderful love stories, readers can escape to a world where love conquers all, the tenderness of a first kiss sweeps you away, and your heart pounds at the sight of the one you love.

When you put it all together, you find romance in its truest form.

Love always finds a way.

Elizabeth North

Executive Director
Dreamspinner Press

K.C. Wells

THE SENATOR'S SECRET

PUBLISHED BY

Published by
DREAMSPINNER PRESS

5032 Capital Circle SW, Suite 2, PMB# 279,
Tallahassee, FL 32305-7886 USA
www.dreamspinnerpress.com

This is a work of fiction. Names, characters, places, and incidents either
are the product of author imagination or are used fictitiously, and any
resemblance to actual persons, living or dead, business establishments,
events, or locales is entirely coincidental.

The Senator's Secret
© 2016 K.C. Wells.

Cover Art
© 2016 Bree Archer.
http://www.breearcher.com
Cover content is for illustrative purposes only and any person depicted
on the cover is a model.

ISBN: 978-1-63477-529-8
Digital ISBN: 978-1-63477-530-4
Library of Congress Control Number: 2016910823
Published September 2016
v. 1.0

Printed in the United States of America
(∞)
This paper meets the requirements of
ANSI/NISO Z39.48-1992 (Permanence of Paper).

Born and raised in the north-west of England, **K.C. WELLS** always loved writing. Words were important. Full stop. However, when childhood gave way to adulthood, the writing ceased, as life got in the way.

K.C. discovered erotic fiction in 2009, when the purchase of a ménage storyline led to the startling discovery that reading about men in love was damn hot. In 2012, arriving at a really low point in life led to the desperate need to do something creative. An even bigger discovery waited in the wings—writing about men in love was even hotter....

K.C. now writes full-time and is loving every minute of her new career.

The laptop still has no idea of what hit it... it only knows that it wants a rest, please. And it now has to get used to the idea that where K.C goes, it goes.

And as for those men in love that she writes about? The list of stories just waiting to be written is getting longer... and longer....

K.C. loves to hear from readers.

E-mail: k.c.wells@btinternet.com
Facebook: www.facebook.com/KCWellsWorld
Twitter: @K_C_Wells
Website: www.kcwellsworld.com

For Lynn.

Acknowledgments

THANK you to my wonderful betas: Jason, Helena, Mardee, Will, and Lynn.

Chapter One

SENATOR Samuel Dalton shivered in the chill wind that whistled by him as he got out of his car to walk to the campaign office. The temperature—around the fifty-degree mark—wasn't that cold for the tail end of January in Raleigh, but it was cool enough that he needed his warm, thick coat against the stiff breeze. He didn't mind it so much; he knew there was a pot of coffee waiting for him.

Sam clutched the shopping bag in his hand and smiled to himself.

Becky is going to love me.

He arrived at the beautiful house on Richmond Run Drive and climbed the three steps to the ornate front door. Not for the first time, he considered his good fortune to work in such a gorgeous space. Mrs. Donnelly rented her former family home to their campaign every year, and Sam loved the house.

He walked into the hall and stuck his head around the door of the first room on his left, which served as the base for the telemarketers. Most of the tables were already occupied with people engaged in calls and making notes, their voices bright and cheerful.

A chorus of "Good morning, Senator" greeted him.

"Good morning, people," he called with a smile. "Isn't it a beautiful day too?" The morning sunlight spilled in through the large windows.

He withdrew and headed up the staircase to the second floor, where four of the five bedrooms served as offices. Curtis's door was closed, but Sam caught the low rumble of his chief of staff's voice. The smallest bedroom was the office of Josh Mapleton, his PR man. Sam peered around the door to see Josh leaning back in his chair, talking on the phone in an animated fashion. Sam shook his head. It was rare to catch Josh when he *wasn't* talking.

He entered his office to find his secretary, Becky Watson, already going through his agenda for the day.

She glanced up as he came into the spacious room, and grinned. "How do you always manage to arrive just as the coffee machine finishes brewing?"

Sam shrugged. "What can I say? It's a gift." He placed his bag on the neat, ordered desk and took off his coat.

Becky was at his side in an instant. "Here, give that to me. I'll hang it up and bring you some coffee." She promptly disappeared through the door that led to her office.

"Have I told you lately that you're a national treasure?" he called after her, glancing through his diary to remind himself of the day's engagements.

"Not often enough, if you ask me."

Sam laughed. He removed the box from his bag and followed her into her small but immaculate office, where every available flat surface had a plant. It was a sea of green in there. He took one look at her desk and groaned. "Seriously? A *Will & Grace* mug?" A new one, it had a photo of Will, Grace, Karen, and Jack, and was by no means the only piece of merchandise from the show that could be seen in her office. "Becky, *how* many years has it been since that show ended? Can't you let it go, let it die a peaceful death—and let all its memorabilia die with it?"

Becky turned, coffee pot in hand, and narrowed her gaze. "Am I asking you to drink from my *Will & Grace* mug? Well?"

"Well, no, but—"

"Then hush," she said immediately, scowling.

Sam arched his eyebrows. "Is that any way to speak to your boss? Especially one who happens to be a state senator, but more importantly in your case, has in his hand a box of your favorite pastries? A box that he bought just for you from that bakery you love over on South Main Street?" He held up the pretty pink box.

Becky stared. "You didn't. Really?" Gone was the scowl. She almost bounced over to him, her face alight with glee. "Aw, you shouldn't have."

When her eager fingers were within inches of the box, Sam snatched it out of her reach and gave her an evil smile. "Maybe next time you'll think twice before you sass me, hmm?"

"He's just bent out of shape because you're not drinking from one of our campaign mugs," Curtis Tucker said as he came through the door, smirking.

Becky snorted. "What—the ones with his face on them? Why on Earth would I want one of those? If I want to see that face, all I have to do is open a door." She turned to Sam, all puppy-dog eyes, batting her lashes. "Can I have my pastries now? Pretty please?"

Sam laughed and handed her the box. "Enjoy."

Becky had been his personal secretary for the last six years, and while her taste in TV merchandise was sometimes questionable, he couldn't fault her work ethic or her loyalty. A middle-aged housewife whose kids had all grown up and gone to college, she'd joined his team when her husband had died, mostly due to the need to get herself out of the house.

"You ready for our meeting?" Curtis asked, helping himself to coffee.

"I will be when Becky finishes doing what she came in here for," Sam said pointedly.

Becky halted, hand already inside the box. "Oops. You go on in and talk to Curtis. I'll bring the coffee in."

Sam walked out of the room, chuckling. "I'm having a case of déjà vu here." He sat at his desk, and Curtis took the chair facing it, mug in hand. "Good morning, by the way."

"Is it?" Curtis remarked dryly.

"Oh Lord, what now?" Sam knew that tone.

"Our friendly neighborhood pastor has been very active over the weekend."

Sam let out a sigh. "What's he been saying now?" Pastor Floyd Hartsell was a particular thorn in Sam's side. "Wasn't there a meeting for the NCTVPC on Saturday?" He'd had no time to follow the ramblings of the North Carolina Traditional Values Policy Council; his weekend had been taken up with the store. It seemed January had brought with it the usual glut of people deciding to renovate their homes, and business at the hardware store had been very brisk.

"Oh, there was indeed," Curtis said with a grimace. "I'm not sure whether Hartsell was speaking as your opponent for reelection or as one of their supporters, but you can guess the rest."

"Hmm, let me see." Sam counted off on his fingers. "Proposing yet another bill threatening to overturn the SCOTUS decision. Talking about the sanctity of marriage. How corruption is rife in our nation. The threat to our state's youth. The—"

"Yeah, all right. Just pick one of them and he voiced off about it." Curtis shook his head. "I know anyone can run for office, but *Jesus*, he gets under my skin."

"But why?" Sam asked, widening his eyes in an affectation of innocence. "He's an honest man, remember? Wholesome image, a family guy, always talking about trust, beliefs…." He bit back his smile. "Honestly, he needs to get himself a new speech writer, because I think we've already heard everything his present one has to offer—at least three times."

The door opened and Becky entered, carrying a mug and a plate with a delicious-looking pastry. She placed them on the desk in front of Sam, favored him with a flash of a smile, and then disappeared back into her office, closing the door behind her.

Sam sipped his coffee. "Anyway, don't spoil my morning regaling me with Hartsell's weekend activities. What about yours? I'm sure I'd find them much more interesting." He grinned.

"Oh, not much to report," Curtis said with a nonchalant air. "Except that I went on a date." His eyes sparkled. "JoAnn. Twenty-seven. Blonde. Stacked. Teacher. And most *definitely* eager to please."

Sam stared at him. "You find time to date? And *please*, do not regale me with the more intimate details of your conquests."

Curtis guffawed. "We're not all monks like you, you know, dedicated to our political careers."

"Something's not right about this picture," Sam grumbled. "Why is it you can't stand up and make a speech in front of a whole load of teachers, but you *can* go out to a club and dance your ass off with those same people?"

Curtis sighed. "We've been through this. I'm not the speechmaker, remember? You've always been more extroverted than me, even in college. In high school too, come to think of it. That's why *you're* the one with his face everywhere." He grinned. "Speaking of which, Josh tells me you topped another poll this weekend."

"Oh Lord, do I want to hear this?" Sam said with a groan.

The voltage of Curtis's grin hadn't diminished in the slightest. "It seems they ran a poll of female voters, asking them which state senators they found particularly… attractive." He waggled his eyebrows. "Is that the third or fourth time now you've been at the top of such a poll?"

"I've lost count," Sam growled.

Curtis chuckled. "Hey, don't knock it. This is why you have a higher profile than most normal senators— it's the way you appeal to a female audience."

"Ironic, huh?"

Curtis shrugged. "It was the same thing in college. You were always more outgoing. I'm more your 'behind the scenes' kinda guy, you know—all about the statistics, the one who kicks people's asses when they don't do what they should…." He smiled. "Seventeen years we've been friends. Jeez, you'd think you'd know me by now." He tilted his head. "And no one says you have to be a monk, you know."

Sam huffed out a breath. "Not this again. We've talked about this. We—"

"No, *I've* talked about this. *You* have ignored my advice." Curtis straightened in his chair and glanced toward the two doors that led from the office before speaking. "Sam. SCOTUS changed everything." His voice was soft. "You could come out now."

Sam put down his mug and met Curtis's earnest gaze. "Dating isn't on my list of priorities. You know what I'm working for. You, more than any other person here. Four years from now, where do I want to be? Hmm?"

"I know, I know, the federal representative. I know Greg Miller is talking about retiring, stepping down as NC's US Senator, and I know you're working with him on this, but Jesus, Sam, you need a life too. All you have is your work as the state senator and your hardware store. You deserve some happiness too." He locked eyes with Sam. "You never dated in college either."

Sam snorted. "Oh, come on. We both knew why I chose to study politics and international affairs, right? This was always the goal. Why the hell would I jeopardize that by dating someone who could feasibly come out of the woodwork at some point in the future and announce to the world, 'Hey! I dated Senator Sam Dalton in college!'"

"Would being out be so bad?"

"Curtis." Sam made sure he had his full attention. "It's okay, really. I've coped this long without a relationship. I can cope a bit longer." He took a long drink of coffee and a bite of his pastry before continuing. "So, how about we leave this topic of conversation and discuss what's on the agenda for this week?"

"Sure," Curtis said resignedly. He pulled out his iPhone and scrolled down the screen.

Sam listened to the list of engagements, not really taking them in. His mind was on their conversation. No way was he about to let Curtis know his real feelings on the issue. No matter what he might say, the truth was Sam was tired of being alone. But he'd spoken the truth. He wasn't about to jeopardize his political career just because he wanted a guy to share his life, his aspirations, and, of course, his bed.

He'd been a late bloomer when it came to his sexual orientation. Sam was twenty when he'd realized girls simply left him cold. The only person he'd ever told that had been his college roommate and friend from high school, Curtis Tucker. Of course, the first thing out of Curtis's mouth had been a demand to know if Sam had the hots for him.

Sam was happy to put him straight on that score. Curtis didn't do it for him either.

Oh, there had been guys who'd piqued his interest over the years, but Sam had steered clear, his eyes constantly on the political prize. But it did make for a lonely existence. Not to mention there was a whole lot of curiosity going on in his head. He had a feeling that if Curtis ever found out just how inexperienced Sam was, he'd march Sam to the nearest gay bar and hook him up with the first available guy.

That was *not* how Sam intended to lose his virginity.

Just the thought sent flames of embarrassment spreading through him like wildfire. How did anyone get to the age of thirty-three and still hold a V card? It went beyond the realms of dedication.

When Curtis cleared his throat, Sam was brought back into the present. "Are we done?"

Curtis lifted his brows. "Well, that depends how much you actually took in of what I just said." He smirked. "Because from where I'm sitting, you were off in your own little world."

Sam had had enough lectures for one day. *And we've barely gotten started.* Things were not looking promising for the rest of his Monday. He reached into his desk and fished out a packet of cigarettes. "You know what? I need a smoke." He didn't fail to notice Curtis's grimace. "Yeah, I know, filthy habit. I've been meaning to quit, but it's not like I smoke a pack a day, right? I'm lucky if I manage one or two around here." Most of the staff were ardent nonsmokers, and Mrs. Donnelly had been very specific on the point of smoking in the house. Sam usually snuck out to the back porch.

"No wonder you haven't got a boyfriend," Curtis said under his breath. "Who'd want to kiss an ashtray?"

Without a word Sam got up from his chair and left the office. He headed down the staircase and out through the kitchen to the back porch. As he opened the door, he caught a delighted, "Yes!"

Gary something—at least Sam thought his name was Gary—one of the telemarketers, was staring at his phone, an expression of utter joy on his face, a cigarette in his other hand.

"Glad someone's having a good day," Sam said with a smile.

"Shit." Gary froze. "Sorry, Senator, I didn't know you were—"

"It's fine," Sam said with a wave of his hand, the one containing the cigarette pack. "I just needed a breath of air and a smoke, which I suppose is sort of a contradiction in terms."

Gary chuckled. "Yeah, just a bit." He went back to staring at his phone, that grin still evident.

Sam watched him for a second. "Okay, I'll bite. What's got you so happy? If it's something you can share."

"Oh, totally." Gary pocketed his phone. "See, right now I'm studying veterinary medical technology, and I just found out I've been accepted to NC State College of Veterinary Medicine. Isn't that awesome?" His face radiated happiness.

"That is amazing news," Sam agreed. "I am so happy for you." On impulse he stepped forward and gave Gary a quick hug, patting his back.

Gary responded instantly and returned his hug. When Sam released him, Gary took a drag of his cigarette and blew a stream of smoke into the air. He gazed at the cigarette held between two fingers. "You know what? Considering how much my tuition is going to cost, maybe it's time to think about giving these babies up for good."

Sam huffed. "You and me both." He gave Gary a grin. "How about we both quit? We've got two months until the primaries. Think we could stop totally by then?" That would please Curtis no end, as well as giving him one less thing to complain about.

"You're on," Gary said, smiling broadly. "Hey, we could encourage each other. They say it's easier if you do it with a buddy."

Sam arched his eyebrows, amused, and Gary's face flushed.

"I'm sorry, Senator, that was really forward of me."

Sam laughed. "It's fine. So if you're going to be my quitting-smoking buddy, what's your name?"

"Gary Mason, sir." He held out his hand, but Sam ignored it.

"Oh, we're past 'sir'—we've hugged already." Gary snickered and Sam smiled. "And it's Sam, okay? But only when it's just us, you got that?"

"I got it." Gary's expression was still joyful. He looked down at his cigarette. "You know what? I'm not even going to finish this." He dropped it to the ground and stubbed it out with his shoe. Then he picked up the butt and dropped it in the trashcan.

"Seeing as you're leading by example," Sam said with a smile, "I shall go one better and not even light up." Not that a cigarette wouldn't feel great right then, but Gary's enthusiasm was infectious.

"Way to go, si—I mean, Sam." The tips of Gary's ears were bright red. He glanced toward the house. "I'd better get back to work. Someone has to call all these people and make sure you get reelected, right?" His eyes gleamed.

Sam laughed. "Yeah, I'd appreciate that." He patted Gary on the back. "Keep up the good work."

"You got it." Gary flashed him one last smile before heading back into the house.

Sam waited until he was alone and then drew in a lungful of clean, cold air. *It was about time I quit anyhow.*

The thought of that unfinished pastry on his desk was like a siren call.

Chapter Two

Monday night

SAM was in that blissful state of warm drowsiness that was usually the precursor to falling asleep on the couch. The fire had died down and now only embers glowed there. He lifted his head from the cushion and stared at the room. Something was different.

When his phone began to vibrate its way across the coffee table, he had his answer.

He glanced at the screen before connecting. Curtis wasn't prone to making late-night phone calls. "Hey, what's up?"

A sigh filled his ears. "You need to see something."

Sam was bolt upright in an instant. "Okay, what's wrong?" He recognized that tone. He didn't get to hear it all that frequently, thank God, but there was no mistaking it.

"Got your laptop handy?"

Sam reached for it and flipped it open. "Yup. What am I looking for?"

Another sigh. "Floyd Hartsell's Facebook page. His campaign page, not his profile."

Sam groaned. "For God's sake, now what?" He pulled up the page and—

"What the *fuck*?"

He was staring at photos of himself.

To be more exact, one photo of him hugging Gary. Another of the two of them laughing and smiling. But what really caught his attention was the post that accompanied it.

What exactly is the nature of the relationship between State Senator Samuel Dalton and one of his staff, captured in this photo taken this morning at the back of Dalton's campaign offices? They say the camera never lies, right? What does this photo say to you?

And maybe now we understand why the senator has been so supportive of SCOTUS's decision last year.

The comments below had already reached more than a hundred. Sam skimmed through them, enough so that he caught the gist: people expressing surprise/outrage/shock that their senator was a closet gay; remarks about him not being a good example to the state's youth; comments about not being able to trust someone who hides his sexuality; and on, and on, and....

He peered at the photos. "Where were these taken from?"

"As far as I can make out without going to the house, they're from the property next door, probably taken from a bedroom window." Curtis paused. "I have to ask this. I've just checked up on this Gary Mason. This is the first time he's worked for us. He's a doctoral student, lives in Raleigh, single. Personable, good at talking to people. Any chance he's been put up to this by Hartsell's crowd? Because the chances of them having someone ready to take a photo when you just *happened* to be down there sharing a cigarette break, and he just *happened* to hug you? And yeah, about that...." Curtis cleared his throat. "Anything you want to tell me, Sam?"

Sam gave a low growl. "Absolutely nothing. Today was the first time I actually spoke with the guy. And as for the hug, he'd just been accepted to vet school, and he was over the moon. It was an *impulse*, for God's sake." He recalled Gary's manner, the way he'd spoken. "As for the likelihood that he's a plant? Uh-uh, I don't buy it. He seemed like a pretty genuine guy." He scraped his fingers across his scalp. "You think he's seen this?"

"Ha! The only reason *you're* seeing it is because Josh never stops trolling the Internet for you. He called me as soon as he saw it. So unless Gary is a fan of Hartsell, has friends who are supporters of Hartsell, or is an insomniac who can't keep off Facebook, then no, I don't think he'll have seen it." Another pause. "Did you notice that post doesn't claim to be written by Hartsell?"

"No, it'll have been posted by one of his minions. He'll be sure to keep his hands clean on this one." Sam sagged into the couch. "So now what?"

Curtis laughed. "Now nothing. You go to sleep. There's nothing you can do about it at this hour. In the morning we'll put the wheels in motion. Want to bet Josh is already on it?"

In spite of his anxiety, that brought a wry smile to Sam's face. "You'd win that bet." Josh was their best find ever. Still, the thought of doing nothing.... "You sure there's nothing I can do? I could go onto his—"

"*You* are going to do nothing but get some sleep, do you hear me?" Curtis's voice was low but firm. "Let us do our jobs, Sam, all right?"

"I hear you," Sam said, albeit with reluctance. "See you in the morning."

Curtis chuckled. "I'll have Becky make the coffee double strength. Good night, boss." He ended the call.

Sam closed the lid of his laptop, his mind in a whirl.

I do not *need this!*

Being in politics was all Sam had ever wanted to do. He wasn't in it for the fame—because hell, there were times when he wished for a life out of the media's glare—but out of a genuine desire to do something for the people of North Carolina. He'd seen too many politicians who oozed sincerity, from whose tongues dripped all the right words, but when it came down to it? They didn't have their constituents' best interests at heart; they were in it for what *they* could get out of it.

Sam loved it when a customer at the store would take him aside and thank him for something he'd done—a policy he'd introduced, a charity he'd supported, or a scandal he'd exposed. He loved that his neighbors felt comfortable enough to walk right up to him on the street and demand to know what he was going to do about such-and-such an issue—and that they did it because they knew he'd do something about it.

And for Pastor Floyd Hartsell, a man who proclaimed himself a Christian, to be such a hate-stirrer, even if he hid it behind the facade of supporting traditional family values....

Is it any wonder I've stayed in the closet? Sam had never wanted to hide, but he was a realist. He'd only been a senator for six years, but he'd seen enough to realize that coming out would *not* do him any favors. The thought that his constituents might view him differently once they knew about his sexual orientation had crossed his mind many times. He hadn't wanted to deal with the fallout.

Well, it looks like that ship has sailed.

Sam had a feeling sleep was going to be pretty elusive.

SAM stepped into the wide hallway and listened. All was quiet. He'd expected to be the first one there, but Curtis's car was already parked out front, along with a couple of others. Then he caught the aroma that wafted down the staircase. The coffee was on, apparently.

He went upstairs and into his office to find it already occupied. Curtis and Josh were deep in conversation, while Becky handed them coffee before retreating into her office.

Sam shrugged off his coat and placed it on a hanger. "Anyone going to wish me a good morning?" He knew he sounded cranky, but after a night of restless tossing and turning, with only a couple of hours' sleep, that was to be expected.

"I would if it were," Curtis remarked dryly. He peered intently at Sam. "Jesus, you look like I feel." He hollered to Becky, "Better bring in the biggest mug you've got, girl. Looks like we're gonna need it this morning."

Becky bustled into the office, a huge mug of steaming coffee in her hand. She took one look at Sam's face and pursed her lips. "Oh my. Here, drink this, and then we'll decide what to do about that no-good, lying piece of sh—"

Sam cleared his throat pointedly, and she snapped her mouth shut. He leaned forward and kissed her cheek. "I appreciate the support, but we will not sink to his level, okay?"

She flushed.

Sam pointed to her office. "Now go get your iPad and be ready to take notes, because I'm sure Josh is already on the case. Right, Josh?" He gave his PR man an expectant glance as he came around to sit at his desk, coffee in hand.

Josh grinned and handed him a sheet of paper. "You know it. This is your statement refuting his claims, ready to go. I've already had a call from the *News & Observer*, asking for our reactions before they go to press. I told them they'd have to wait for your official statement." He gazed speculatively at Sam. "We *can* refute it, right, Sam? I mean, there's no truth in it, right?"

Sam locked gazes with Josh. "I am not now, nor have I ever been, in a relationship with Gary Mason. That clear enough for you?"

"Gotcha." Josh gave him a sheepish smile. "I had to ask."

"This really burns me, you know?" Becky piped up as she came through the door, iPad in her hand. "Does that Pastor Hartsell think he can just go around, making up shit like this?" She glared at Curtis. "He can't go around telling everyone Sam is gay when we know he's not!"

Curtis's eyes flickered in Sam's direction before he spoke. "Only, Hartsell didn't say that, did he?" he chided Becky gently.

Josh snorted. "Yeah, he was real careful about how that post was worded. '*What is the nature of the relationship...?*' And the part asking folks what that photo said to them? Inspired. His supporters come up with all the shit he wouldn't dare say. And of course, he doesn't comment on any of it." He scowled. "He doesn't need to; they went ahead and said it all for him. He gets to sit back and read it, while *we're* the ones doing the weeping." Josh stuck out his chin. "So let's get this statement out. He won't be so cocky when we're suing his ass for libel and defamation of character."

"You sure we want to go that route?" Curtis said quietly.

Sam fired him a look, but Curtis was avoiding his gaze.

"Of *course* he does," Becky interjected, her eyes flashing. "Sam can't just sit here and let that... *man* hint that he's... well, it's just...." She narrowed her eyes. "You know what would cook his goose? If we announced that Sam *was* gay, and that he and this Gary were secretly engaged. That'd make Hartsell look like a nasty piece of work, outing Sam like that and making him look all sleazy, when they were keeping it quiet so as not to detract from the campaign." She gave Curtis an evil grin. "Yeah, they'd look all wholesome—a sweet, cute gay couple heading for marriage, and there's him, trying to make the whole situation seem sordid."

There was a stunned silence.

Sam was the first to react. "This is *not* the plot from a *Will & Grace* episode, all right?" His head was still reeling from her suggestion.

"Wait a minute, wait a minute!" Josh straightened in his chair, his eyes shining. "You might have something there."

Two heads swiveled in his direction, and from three mouths came the same word simultaneously: "What?"

Josh was nodding, his cheeks flushed. "This might work to our advantage."

"Excuse me?" Sam was having a hard time dealing with this.

"Oh, come on," Josh said with a cheeky grin. "Coming out is fashionable these days. *Everybody's* doing it—actors, athletes, singers…. Since the SCOTUS decision last year, coming out is the new black." He waggled his eyebrows. "It'd bring you a whole heap of new supporters, Sam."

What the…?

Becky was on the edge of her seat. "Yeah. Let everyone see them as a committed couple, putting their relationship on hold until after the election. They've not been *hiding* it, exactly—they just want the focus to be on politics."

"But—" The turn in the discussion left Sam gaping in amazement.

Josh waved a hand to hush him. "Yeah," he said, nodding excitedly. "I like that. We do a press conference, break the story, get public opinion on our side, sympathy for the way Hartsell has portrayed their relationship—"

"*What* relationshi—"

Becky and Josh ignored Sam, lost in their own little world. "Oh my God!" Becky put her hand to her chest. "Can you imagine? The wedding? It would be so beautiful!"

"Wedding? *What* wed—"

"We'd have lots of photos taken of the happy couple, showing their life together. We could start up a Twitter account where they send cute little tweets to each other." Josh grinned. "Move over, Neil Patrick Harris and David Burtka, Elton John and David Furnish, Ellen and Portia—they could become *the* gay couple of the decade."

"Okay, that's enough!" Sam growled. When his staff jumped and turned to face him, he pointed to the outer door of his office. "You two," he said, indicating Josh and Becky, "out, now."

Becky gave him a startled glance before lurching to her feet and scooting out of the room, Josh following her with a perplexed expression.

Sam closed the door behind them and faced his chief of staff. "What. The. Fuck, Curtis?" He glared at his friend, his heart pounding, head aching.

Curtis regarded him calmly. "What have I been telling you?"

Sam stared at him, mouth open. "You... you're not actually *considering* their harebrained scheme, are you?"

He shrugged. "Why not?"

"Why not?" Sam threw his hands up in the air. "Amendment One, *that's* why not! Have you forgotten that 61 percent of NC voters backed the amendment to define marriage as being an institution between a man and a woman in 2012?"

"No, I've not forgotten." That calm air hadn't left him. "But let's look at the figures, shall we? The population of North Carolina back then was an estimated 9.7 million. Do you know how many voters backed the amendment? A staggering 1,317,178. Only 840,802 voters opposed it. That means roughly 13 percent of the state's population cast ballots in favor of the amendment."

"My point exactly!" Sam said with a triumphant air.

"Sam, there were 6.6 million registered voters in the state. That leaves the opinions of at least three million voters unaccounted for. And times are changing. A recent Elon University Poll found 45 percent of voters supported same-sex marriage, as opposed to 43 percent who are against it." Curtis smiled. "Josh is right. You may find yourself with a whole new set of supporters if you do this."

"Ah, right, I'm glad you brought that point up." Sam folded his arms across his chest. "*If* I do this. There are a bunch of variables that no one seems to be taking into consideration."

"Such as?"

"Have you even considered the fact that this is a lie? There *is* no relationship."

"But there could be," Curtis said simply.

Sam sank into his chair. "What? It takes two to have a relationship, last time I looked."

"And sometimes three," Curtis added with a grin.

Sam shook his head. "Just keep your mind on the problem we have here. Those two," he said, pointing to the door, "are already planning a huge gay wedding when one half of the engaged couple is straight."

"You know that for sure?" Curtis arched his eyebrows.

"Well, no, but…." Sam struggled to maintain his composure.

"Think about it. We'd be asking Gary to go through a marriage ceremony. He'd know it was a publicity stunt. And he'd only have to stay married to you for two to four years. That would be long enough for appearance's sake. After that he could ask for a divorce."

"Why the fuck would he even agree to such a thing?"

Curtis shrugged. "We make it worth his while. The way I figure it, he's a student, so that means loans, tuition…. We could offer to pay off everything, leaving him free and clear of debt." He tilted his head. "You think that might be a big enough incentive to consider this?"

"But you know nothing about him!" Sam yelled. "For all you know, he might be in a committed relationship."

Curtis eyed him, that air of calm still apparent. "The personal information he filed with us says not. Of course, he could be keeping it quiet, but we'd be sure to ask that up front."

Sam snorted. "Well, *duh*, seeing as you'd be asking him to give up any chance of a personal life for *how many* years?" He put his elbows on the desk, his head in his hands, and heaved a sigh. "Curtis, I'm sorry, but this… this doesn't feel right. Don't you think that lying like this makes me just as bad as Hartsell and his supporters?"

Curtis got up from his chair, came to stand next to Sam, and leaned against the desk. He placed his hand on Sam's shoulder and spoke in a low voice. "Hartsell has put it out there that you might be gay. Now, while there is absolutely *nothing wrong* with being gay, it changes things. For one thing, if you deny it, and it comes out later that you lied, that doesn't look good. And even if you *do* deny it, there are going to be people who think there's no smoke without fire, and you'll be under constant scrutiny."

Sam said nothing. He knew Curtis was right.

"But what Josh is proposing is a way out. Yes, it would be a lie, but it would have positive effects. You'd be able to live for the first time as an openly gay man. You'd probably have a lot of public sympathy after this. And yeah, you might gain more voters. We're trying to turn a negative into a positive here, Sam." He rubbed Sam's shoulder. "The only thing I can think of that would prevent this from working would be if Gary doesn't go for it."

Sam slowly raised his head. "Then I guess we'd better get him in here and find out."

Curtis stared. "You mean…."

Sam sat back in his chair. "I mean nothing. Let's see what Gary has to say first, okay? Because if he says no, that blows this whole plan out of the water."

Curtis nodded. "I'll go see if he's arrived yet." He walked toward the office door, but paused as he reached it. "And Sam?"

Sam met his gaze. "Yeah?"

"Whatever happens, I'm right here with you, okay?"

Sam smiled. "I never doubted that for a second. And can I just say something? You having all those figures at your fingertips was pretty damn impressive."

Curtis grinned. "This *is* what you pay me for, right?"

Sam clutched his chest. "I pay you?" When Curtis groaned, he waved him off. "Now go find my would-be fiancé."

Curtis nodded and left the room.

Sam leaned his head against the back of his chair and closed his eyes.

This is just… nuts.

Chapter Three

Tuesday

FIVE minutes passed before Curtis returned. Five long minutes that gave Sam the opportunity to reconsider the whole preposterous idea.

What am I thinking?

It would never work. In the world of politics, secrets never got to stay secret forever. The truth always came to light in the end. And something like this? The odds on it staying a secret for long were astronomically low.

No, the best thing that could happen would be for Gary to listen to their plan and then laugh in their faces to show them just how ridiculous the whole idea was. That would leave Sam with the issue of Hartsell's post and the resultant fallout.

Guess I'll just have to face the music.

The door opened and Curtis walked in, with Gary behind him.

To his surprise, Gary nudged past Curtis and approached his desk, his hands clasped in front of him. His cheeks were flushed, his chin lowered to his chest. "I am so, so sorry, Senator. I can understand completely why you're angry. A friend of mine messaged me this morning, sending me the link to that post. I had no idea there was anyone with a camera on us. Please, you have to believe me."

Sam stared in amazement at Gary's obvious embarrassment, then fired Curtis a look. "Did you tell Gary why he's in here?" he demanded.

Curtis shook his head. "I just said you wanted to see him." From his position behind Gary, Curtis held up his hands defensively, his eyes wide.

Damn it. The poor guy thought he was in trouble.

"Gary, sit down, please." Sam indicated the chair facing his desk. "I swear, you're not in trouble. Far from it." His stomach churned at the thought of Gary believing Sam was angry with him.

"I… I'm not?" Gary frowned. "I don't understand."

"Gary, can I get you a cup of coffee?" Curtis asked.

"Coffee? Yeah, sure. Thanks, Mr. Tucker." Gary appeared confused. As an afterthought, he added, "Black, please. No sugar."

Curtis patted his arm and disappeared into Becky's office.

"The reason you're here is because Josh Mapleton, who is in charge of PR, has come up with a rather unusual proposal, and it involves you."

"Really?"

Curtis appeared, carrying a mug of coffee. "That stuff will keep you on your toes," he said with a smile. He dragged another chair up and sat next to Gary. "Okay, Gary. We know you've seen Pastor Hartsell's Facebook post."

Gary nodded and took a sip of his coffee. "Whoa, you weren't kidding about the coffee, were you?"

Curtis snickered but then straightened his face. "The thing is, while it's true you and Senator Dalton aren't… involved with each other, the pastor has accidentally hit on something that *is* true. I'm going to share that with you, because it will help with what comes next."

Sam sighed. "You don't have to sugarcoat it, Curtis." He turned to Gary. "What my well-meaning chief of staff is trying to say is, I'm… I'm gay."

Gary stared at him in silence for so long, the hairs stood up along Sam's arms. "*You're* gay?"

His inflection caught Sam off guard. "Yes," he said slowly, drawing out the syllable.

"See," Gary said after a moment's pause, "*this* is why I thought I was in trouble. I thought you'd figure I was some sort of plant, put in here to entrap you."

"Why would I think that?" Sam asked.

"Because… I'm gay too." He looked from Sam to Curtis and back to Sam again. "You didn't know?"

"Uh-uh." Sam's head was spinning. *What are the odds on this?*

"And the only people who know the senator is gay are in this room," Curtis said quietly. He glanced at Sam. "Although that might be subject to change."

Sam leaned forward, his arms on his desk. "And going back to what I said yesterday morning? I'm Sam, okay?"

Gary nodded and then took a drink of his coffee. "So, what's this unusual proposal?"

Sam regarded Curtis, who shook his head. The ball was in Sam's court, it appeared.

He took a moment to collect his thoughts. "The feeling around here is that we try to turn Pastor Hartsell's little Facebook post to our advantage, thus minimizing the damage." He paused. Gary was watching him intently, his hands wrapped around his mug. Sam sighed. "This is going to sound crazy, but the PR department had the idea that voters would be more sympathetic and less inclined to criticize me for hiding my sexuality if it was announced that you and I were… secretly engaged."

Gary's jaw dropped and his eyes were huge.

Sam took a deep breath and forged ahead. "We tell them we've been keeping a low profile because we didn't want to deflect attention away from the election."

Gary arched his eyebrows. "Engaged?" he said at last.

"If we do it this way, Hartsell comes across in a negative light," Curtis added. "We make your relationship legitimate, wholesome, sweet…. We show you planning your wedding, sharing your lives, that kind of thing. You two are the injured party. You're in a committed relationship, letting Sam focus on his job, whereas Hartsell is trying to score points off Sam by making him look sleazy and sordid."

Gary was still staring at them open-mouthed, his coffee forgotten.

"Of course, we wouldn't expect you to do this for nothing," Curtis said quickly. "To show our appreciation, we would pay off all your student loans, plus we'd pay all the tuition for vet school. You could graduate free from debt."

Gary sagged in his chair. "Whoa. My God. Seriously?"

Both Sam and Curtis nodded.

Gary put his mug on the desk and sat up straight. "Okay, a couple of points. You say 'engaged.' What would that entail?"

Sam gaped. *Is he really thinking about this?*

"We'd have to come clean about the relationship, of course, so there'd be a press conference. You'd have to be there. Plus you'd have to be seen with Sam on a regular basis. Interviews, photo ops, you accompanying him on his public engagements—that kind of thing." Curtis fell silent, fixing Gary with a thoughtful gaze. "This would be the point where you tell us if there'd be an impediment to this plan, should we decide to go ahead with it. For example, if there was a husband or two lurking in your private life? Kids?"

"No, I'm single, and I'm not dating anyone," Gary said absently, his forehead creased. "And what about this wedding we're supposed to be planning? I assume we're talking after the election? You'd expect me to go through with it?"

Curtis nodded. "For appearance's sake you'd need to remain married for a couple of years at least. After that...." He gave a shrug. "You'd be free to seek a divorce."

"Married," Gary said heavily.

"No one would be asking you to move in with me right this second," Sam added. "We'd just be engaged. For the time being."

"This is why you need to think carefully about this, Gary," Curtis said gently. "It's not just the engagement.

The marriage would mean you giving up on a personal life for as many years as you'd remain married to Sam. No dating, period. Think of the scandal it would cause if the press found out you had a boyfriend."

Gary studied his mug in silence for a moment before picking it up and draining half of its contents. "So let me get this straight. We'd tell the world, '*Hey, you got us. Yes, we're gay. We're also engaged.*' And then we'd make it look good for the cameras. When the election is over, we get married." He peered intently at Sam. "I'm assuming that's whether you win or lose, because if you lose and the wedding is called off, *someone* will call bullshit. And I think we all know who that would be, right?" He smiled. "Of course, you're not going to lose, so that won't be an issue."

Sam was dizzy with it all. Gary's matter-of-fact attitude was not what he'd been expecting.

"And I'd live with you, acting out the role of husband whenever we're in public, and foregoing any possibility of a, quote, 'normal' life for a couple of years at least," Gary added.

Sam stared at him. When it was couched in those terms, Gary would be crazy to say yes, even with their financial incentive. Sam stifled a sigh. Just for a second back there, he'd been hopeful, but after Gary had told it like it really was, Sam knew it just wasn't going to work.

"That's basically it, yes." Curtis pursed his lips. "Okay, we've covered payment, the period of time this would cover, the wedding…." He tapped his fingers on the desk and then smiled. "Oh yes: sex."

Sam blinked. "Excuse me?" He shifted on his chair. Across from him, Gary's mouth had fallen open once more.

Curtis snorted. "Don't you both look at me like I've grown another head or something. If this goes ahead, the pair of you are basically agreeing to two to four years of celibacy. No hookups. Nada. Because living in Asheville? We'd be talking zero anonymity."

Gary cleared his throat. "Look, my last relationship was a year ago, and there hasn't been anyone since. Besides, my studies and setting up my future career take precedence."

Sam nodded. "And I've been so busy, what with my work as senator and running the store, I've had little time for romance." His heart pounded. "As far as I see it, my life would change very little—apart from the fact that I'd gain a husband."

Gary gave a nervous laugh. "Funny how we discuss all those other things, and sex is almost forgotten."

Curtis shrugged. "But it's something that needed discussing."

Sam studied Gary's face, his stomach churning. *This feels so... cold.* He knew the reasoning behind it, but still, they were being so damn *clinical* about the whole thing. Any second now he expected Curtis to mention contracts.

"Of course, if you agree, we'd put everything in writing and you'd sign a contract," Curtis said. "A 'no sex with others' clause would have to form part of the agreement, after all. You could have it checked by a lawyer before making your final decision."

Damn. Sometimes Sam hated being right.

Curtis regarded them both. "So I take it that works for both of you?"

"Sure," Gary murmured.

"Yes, that's fine." It was the last thing Sam wanted to think about right then.

Curtis gazed at Gary. "Any more questions?"

Gary nodded. "Would I carry on working the phones?"

Curtis shook his head. "We haven't had the chance to discuss any of the details with Josh yet, but I think it would be highly unlikely. Once he sets the PR machine into motion, your life won't be your own for a while. That's another thing you need to consider. You'd be living your life in the media spotlight."

"But it'd be just for the cameras," Gary reiterated. "Once we're married, and I assume living together, would I be able to have privacy when it's just us?"

Sam nodded. "My house in Asheville is plenty big enough for the two of us. You'd have your own space. The only thing we'd need to share would be the kitchen."

Gary gave Sam a speculative glance. "As I see it, if we're going to do this, we need to move fast. Otherwise, if we delay, it might look bad, like we needed the time to put this together."

What the fuck? Sam wasn't sure he'd heard right. Because it sounded like Gary was considering it. "*Are* we going to do this?" he asked, his heartbeat racing. "If you need more time to think about it…."

Gary smiled. "No, I don't need more time. You're making it worth my while to do this. I can't tell you what a weight around my neck those student loans have been." He met Sam's gaze head-on. "Yes. I'll do it."

"Be sure about this," Curtis said in a firm tone. "I know it's easy to be blinded by the idea of becoming debt-free, but please, consider all the salient points. We're asking a hell of a lot of you."

Gary regarded Curtis in silence before turning his attention to Sam. He gazed at Sam, and the careful scrutiny sent a shiver down Sam's spine. Not an unpleasant shiver either. Those cool green eyes were appraising Sam, weighing him.

For the first time since Josh had come up with the whole absurd scheme, a tiny part of Sam found himself hoping Gary would say yes.

"Okay, I've thought about it, and the answer is still yes. I'll do it." Gary pushed back his blond hair from his forehead and gave Sam a slight smile. "Consider yourself engaged, Sam."

There was a heavy feeling in Sam's stomach as he took Gary's extended hand and shook it briskly. *This isn't right.* It didn't matter what Curtis said.

Gary sat back and grinned at Curtis. "So what's next?"

Curtis rose. "Next is we break it to Josh that his boss isn't as straight as he thinks he is, and then we sit back and watch a whirlwind in action." When Gary frowned, Curtis snickered. "Trust me. Josh in full flow? Grab on to something and hold on tight." He returned Gary's grin and met Sam's gaze. "I'll go fetch our wedding planners. When I last saw them, they were in the kitchen, trying to work out what they'd done to piss you off." He chuckled. "My God, I can't wait to see Becky's face. She is gonna love this!" With that he left the office.

An awkward silence fell.

What is one supposed to say in a situation like this? Sam was at a loss for words.

Gary cleared his throat. "I guess the first thing on the agenda is you and I need to talk, right? Find out a little about each other?" He smiled. "Especially if your PR guy gets moving fast. I don't want to be caught off guard if I get asked questions."

Sam was grateful one of them was thinking clearly. "That's a good idea. We'll see what Josh has in mind, and then we'll schedule in some time for us to sit down and chat."

The door opened and Josh, Becky, and Curtis entered. Becky arched her eyebrows at the sight of Gary and gave Sam a questioning look.

Curtis closed the door behind them. "Okay, sit down. We need to talk."

GARY closed the back door of the house and leaned against the side of the porch, fingers digging into his pockets for his pack of cigarettes. For some reason his hands were shaking.

Well, duh. It isn't every day I get engaged to a complete stranger.

Okay, so Sam wasn't exactly a stranger, but still…. The whole situation was seriously weird. He was finding it hard to believe he'd actually agreed to it.

Then he remembered: *No debts.*

Yup, that was definitely a good enough reason right there.

Gary took his first drag on the cigarette and closed his eyes. The morning had taken a surreal turn, and he kept expecting to open his eyes and find out it had all been a dream.

He could see why Josh thought it a good idea. When Gary had read Hartsell's post and seen himself in that photo—a totally innocent situation made somehow… dirty by the comments—he'd been sickened. Not so much for himself, but for Sam. Gary genuinely liked the senator. From everything he'd read about Sam, everything he'd heard from those who'd worked on his campaigns in the past, Sam was a really nice guy who cared about people.

The last thing Gary had expected when he arrived at work that morning was to find himself engaged shortly after. Not that it was such a bad position to find himself in. Apart from the financial aspect, there were definitely benefits to being engaged to Senator Sam Dalton.

Like the fact that he was drop-dead gorgeous, for one thing.

Gary pictured Sam. He was taller than Gary, maybe five eleven, with dark brown hair and deep brown eyes. That glimpse of Sam without his jacket just then had been revealing. There were some nicely toned arms hiding under that crisp white shirt, not to mention a lean torso and broad chest. Yeah, a pleasant guy all wrapped up in a handsome package. Spending time with Sam would *not* be a hardship, that was for sure.

Don't get carried away. None of this is real, remember?

That thought was a sobering one. Especially when he remembered he'd be celibate for at least two years.

Better buy shares in hand lotion, then.

Behind him, the door opened, and Gary turned. Sam stood there, his gaze lowered to Gary's hand—and his cigarette.

"Aw, shit." He'd completely forgotten. "Sorry, I just needed one."

Sam snickered. "Yeah, well, that's understandable, given the circumstances. Why do you think I'm out here?" He held up his pack. "Great minds, huh?"

Gary fished out his lighter and held it, hand still trembling slightly, while Sam lit up. "So… what did *you* do this morning?" he said with a smile.

Sam laughed. "Yeah, I know. Unreal, huh?" He took a drag. "I had to get out of there. Josh is going into overdrive."

Gary chuckled. "He's a character, huh? Is he always like that?"

"What—full of energy, acting like he's drunk about twenty cups of coffee? Pretty much." Sam's expression grew more sober. "Look, before we go any further, there's something I have to say."

"Okay," Gary said slowly. Sam's hesitant manner and obvious embarrassment made him wonder what the hell was coming.

"I am so, *so* sorry that we put you in this position," Sam said earnestly. "I know you haven't been with the team all that long, and to have you react like this, well…." He drew in a deep breath. "Let's just say you were more open to the idea than I thought you'd be."

Gary chuckled. "Yeah, I may have surprised myself back there too. But really, there's no apology needed. It wasn't your fault he had someone spying on us. And if I hadn't been out here sneaking a quick smoke, there'd have been nothing to see, right? It was just bad timing." He regarded Sam with interest. "Can I ask you something?"

Sam arched his eyebrows. "Considering what we just agreed to? Ask away."

"How long did it take you to get your head around this whole idea?"

Sam snorted. "What makes you think I have?" He shook his head. "When Josh and Becky first came up with the idea, tossing it back and forth between them, I thought they'd lost it. Then Curtis started talking statistics, appealing to common sense."

Gary nodded slowly. "Let me guess. 'Let's appeal to the gay voters, especially all those who don't follow Hartsell and the NCTVPC.'" He scowled. "I took a peek at their website once. Made me want to puke." He studied Sam. "You sure you want to do this? Because this does seem a pretty drastic way to go."

"To be honest? I'm still not entirely convinced. But what are my options?" Sam puffed on his cigarette. "Becky said it really burned her to see Hartsell's campaign post. Well, it burned me too. You and I, all we were doing was sharing a cigarette and celebrating your news. Nothing remotely seedy or dirty about it, and yet with that one post, he made it look like I had something to hide. The pair of us, skulking in the backyard...."

"Yeah. I felt the same way."

"And don't you think it's time North Carolina had a gay senator?" Sam asked with a smile.

"Sure, but you could still be a gay senator without this... subterfuge."

Sam fell silent for a moment. "What looks better, to come out because Hartsell's forced our hand and left me no choice? Or to do it this way, where I'm still coming out, but at least we get the chance to put a spin on it, to make it sweet, romantic, and nothing like he painted us? Granted, ours is the more desperate option of the two—behind the scenes, at any rate—but ultimately it could mean his nasty little post backfires on him and we gain public sympathy." He sighed. "Both options end up with the same result—Senator Sam Dalton is gay—but you have to admit, this way is more positive."

Gary couldn't argue with that. Then he smiled. "By the way, your secretary seemed awfully happy to hear your news."

Sam guffawed. "What gave it away? That delighted squeal of hers that went ultrasonic?" He shook his head. "You know, if you look up *fag hag* in the dictionary, it says *See Becky Watson.*" Gary let out a smothered gasp, and Sam's cheeks flushed. "That was *her* term for describing herself, before you go thinking I'm insulting her. That woman is *obsessed* with gay men."

Gary laughed. "And now she finds out she has one for a boss. She must be in heaven."

"Oh Lord," Sam groaned. "I didn't think about that part. She'll be in her element." He paused and looked over Gary's shoulder, peering intently at something.

Gary turned to look. "What is it?"

"I was just looking to see if there was a camera trained on us, but then I realized it didn't matter—not with what we're about to break, anyhow." Sam pulled out his phone and glanced at it. "Speaking of which, we'd better go back upstairs. Josh will want to run through the press conference protocol with you before this afternoon."

"This afternoon?" Gary's heartbeat raced.

Sam smiled sweetly. "Did I forget to mention that he's arranged a press conference, which is due to take place in about three hours' time?"

"Yeah, you did," Gary said with a scowl. "I think we're gonna need to work on our communication." He stubbed out his cigarette with his shoe and then picked up the butt. "Looks like I picked the wrong week to quit smoking."

To his relief Sam burst out laughing. "I like it. Looks like we have the same taste in movies too." He held the door open for Gary. "After you."

As they made their way up to Sam's office, Gary realized he'd relaxed a little.

He's got a similar sense of humor. This might work after all.

Chapter Four

Coming Out

"WHERE have you two been?" Josh groused as they came through the door into Sam's office. "Sneaking off together? Don't bury yourselves in the part, guys."

Sam gave him a hard stare. "And don't forget who pays you, Mr. Mapleton."

A flush crept across Josh's cheeks. "Sorry, Sam," he mumbled. "It's just that the phones haven't stopped. They're white-hot."

"Huh?" Sam paused at Becky's doorway and peered inside. "Hey, can we have some—"

A mug was thrust into his hand. "Here you go. I'm just pouring one for Gary."

Sam chuckled. "Becky, you're a—"

"Yeah, yeah, I know, a national treasure," she muttered, waving her hand dismissively. "Now go sit down, drink your coffee, and talk to Josh. You have work to do." Sam stared at her, and she glared. "Get a move on! You have a certain pastor to put in his place, remember? Not to mention a speech to make." She handed him another mug. "Here's Gary's."

Sam took it and went to sit at his desk, shaking his head. He passed the mug to Gary and gestured for him to sit before giving Josh his full attention. "So what was that about the phones?"

"They started ringing about thirty minutes ago," Josh said, "and they're showing no signs of stopping anytime soon. We've told everyone manning the phones to tell all callers there will be a press conference later today, and that they'll get what they're after then and no sooner." He scrolled through his iPhone. "I've had calls from all over the state. It seems someone reposted the photos and Hartsell's campaign post, and it's gone viral." He grinned at Sam and Gary. "You two are big news, it appears." He gazed at their mugs and scowled. "Hey, Becky, where's *my* coffee? I'm the only one who's done any work around here this morning." When Sam caught his eye, he bit his lip. "Sorry, boss."

Curtis snickered. "What was that you said about burying yourself in a part?"

Josh ignored him. "Okay, Curtis and I have gone through your schedule for the rest of this week and we've wiped the board."

Sam paused, mug halfway to his mouth. "You've done what?"

"What about me?" Gary asked. "Am I included in these changes too?"

Curtis laughed. "Don't look at me. This is Josh's shindig now."

"I'm sorry, but you two have some serious catching up to do," Josh told Sam and Gary. "We're about to tell the voters of North Carolina—and judging by the calls, the rest of the US too—that you two have been together for a while. There is *no way* I am letting you anywhere near journalists and interviewers without—"

"Wait a minute," Sam interjected. "Interviewers?"

Josh let out an impatient sigh. "Sam, I've just spent the last half hour setting up interviews, radio broadcasts, TV talk shows, magazine articles—you name it. Everyone wants to know about you and Gary, why you've hidden your sexual orientation, your hopes for the future, your plans...." He grinned. "All publicity is good publicity, right? But they won't be taking place for a few days, or maybe even next week. Like I was saying, I'm not letting you anywhere near those guys until you two have had a chance to become more familiar with each other. Trust me, if you walk into an interview and it becomes obvious that you know diddly squat about each other, someone *will* notice, and then, as Becky observed earlier, our goose will be well and truly cooked."

"But what about my engagements?" Sam demanded. "I was due to do a Q&A at Duke University Tuesday afternoon next week, not to mention a meeting with the Chamber of Commerce, a visit to the county fair...."

"I've postponed the Chamber of Commerce meeting until a later date, and we can lose the county fair visit without anyone batting an eyelid. The Duke event can still go ahead, however, but Gary will be going with you."

Gary blinked but said nothing, sipping his coffee instead.

"So tell me," Sam said, sitting back and folding his arms across his chest, "what am I going to be doing the rest of this week?"

"You and your *fiancé*," Josh said with a gleam in his eye, "will be taking some time away from politics and getting away from it all." He snorted. "Yeah, right. By the time I'm finished with you two, everyone will know exactly what you were doing every minute of every day." He cackled and rubbed his hands together gleefully.

"Why am I getting a bad feeling about this?" Gary murmured. "What about my doctorate?"

Josh gave Gary a hard stare. "I'm sure you can spend a bit of time away from your studies for this."

Gary said nothing, but that frown hadn't gone away.

Sam knew where he was coming from; he was already feeling an uneasy pressure in his belly.

"I've arranged for a photographer to shadow you both," Josh said. "His job will be to take as many pictures as possible. Once we've gotten the story out there, we're going to let the public see you together. Shopping, the movies, going for walks…. All the things an engaged couple should be doing, but with one difference—the photographer gets to record every detail. I want photos of you walking down the street in Raleigh, holding hands. Then we'll tweet them from different accounts to make it look like members of the public took them, you know, with comments like, 'Aww, how sweet!' and 'Don't they make an adorable couple,' et cetera."

Sam had always known Josh was good at his job, but right then he felt like he was staring at an oncoming freight train and there was no way to dodge its path.

"Which reminds me." Josh gazed expectantly at Gary. "I'm assuming there are no horror stories about you just waiting to crawl out of the woodwork? No surprises we need to be aware of, like a husband? Kids? Stuff like that?"

Gary sighed. "No, nothing like that."

"And we already asked him that," Curtis added.

"Any hobbies?"

Gary stared at him. "Josh, I'm too busy working my ass off at my studies to have hobbies. The only time I get away from that is when I volunteer at the Wake County SPCA."

Josh's eyes lit up. "SPCA? Puppies? Kitty-cats?" He grinned and rubbed his hands together briskly. "Photo ops!" His fingers danced over the virtual keypad on his phone.

Gary shifted in his chair, giving Sam sidelong glances, his mouth drawn into a straight line.

Josh appeared not to notice his reaction, plowing on. "So I'm suggesting Gary spends the rest of this week and the weekend at your houses in Raleigh and Asheville, Sam. That will give you two time to get to know each other. We want you relaxed with each other when you're being interviewed, and that kind of rapport can't be achieved overnight." He pursed his lips and gazed at them keenly. "In fact, it might be better if Gary stays with you for longer than that. You two need to be in each other's pockets for at least a week."

Curtis cleared his throat. "A more immediate matter is the press conference. We need to put together a timeline for you, plus some backstory. Because you know the reporters are going to ask all kinds of questions. We need to get your story straight." He smirked. "If you know what I mean."

Sam snickered, but Gary was staring at Curtis with wide eyes. "Will I have to speak?"

Curtis opened his mouth, but Josh got there first. "Other than to say how pleased you are that it's finally out in the open and how happy you are that you can be honest about your relationship? No," he stated emphatically.

"Guess that answers *that* question," Gary muttered under his breath.

"Sam will be doing all the talking," Curtis said. "It's what he's good at. You just get to stand at his side and look supportive. Think you can handle that?"

Gary straightened in his chair. "Sure. I can do that."

Sam felt a pang of sympathy for him. Gary had just been thrust into a world he clearly felt uneasy with. "It'll be fine," Sam assured him. "And it will get easier, I'm positive of it."

Gary gave him a quick smile. "I'm sure you're right."

The thing was, he didn't look sure.

Sam made a promise to himself. He would do everything in his power to ensure Gary had as easy a ride as he could make it. After all, they might be paying for his help, but it was still a huge thing to ask.

"Okay." Josh smiled at Becky as she placed a mug of coffee in front of him. He grabbed his stylus and iPad and gazed at Sam and Gary. "Let's get to work. We have a couple of hours to get you two ready to face your public, and I want you word perfect." He grinned. "I love it when I get to crack the whip."

Curtis said nothing but raised his eyebrows.

Sam had a feeling when this was all over, Josh might regret his present exuberance.

WHEN his phone buzzed, Sam grabbed it instantly. "Josh is already downstairs in the Press room. He says he's ready for us." He glanced across his desk at Gary. "But are *you* ready for this?"

Gary drew in a couple of deep breaths. "As I'll ever be."

Becky stood in the doorway to her office. "You know what? You should walk into the press room holding hands," she cooed.

Curtis growled. "No, they should *not*. This is a press conference, for God's sake, not one of those cute-and-fluffy gay romances you're so fond of reading." When she gasped, he snorted. "Yeah, I see them on your desk. You forget, I see everything." He turned away from her and gestured to the outer door. "Let's go, guys." He winked at Sam. "And don't think I can't see that face you're pulling right this second, Becky."

Sam tried not to laugh when Becky gaped at him.

"How… how did you…?" she stuttered.

Curtis turned back to face her. "Having eyes in the back of my head comes with the job, didn't you know?" He gave her an evil grin. "Well, you do now."

Sam and Gary left the office, with Curtis behind them, still chuckling. "I know she means well, but *Jesus*…. Holding *hands*?" They went down the staircase and into the hallway. Curtis paused at the doorway to the pressroom and faced them. From behind the paneled door came the buzz of many voices.

Sam was no stranger to speaking in front of an audience, so he was surprised to find he had butterflies.

Next to him, Gary was pale. On an impulse Sam rubbed his back. "Hey, it'll be fine. Just remember to breathe, all right?" He gave Gary a hopefully confident smile.

"Okay, deep breath. Let's do this." Curtis opened the door, and they stepped into the maelstrom.

As soon as they crossed the threshold, the cameras began flashing. Sam led Gary to a table set up at one end of the room, microphones waiting for them. In front of the table were rows of seats, about ten in total, and every seat was occupied. At the rear of the room were two guys with video cameras.

Josh stood by the table, smiling politely. Sam and Gary took their seats behind it, and Curtis went to stand at the side, his back to the wall.

Josh held up his hands for silence, and an expectant hush fell over the assembled guests. "Senator Dalton has a brief statement to make," he informed the waiting journalists, "and then he'll take questions from the floor." He gave Sam a nod and went to stand next to Curtis.

Sam smiled at the faces before him. "Good afternoon, ladies and gentlemen. Anyone seen any good photos of me lately?" He grinned, and a wave of laughter rippled through the audience. Beside him, Gary relaxed a little. Sam nodded. "As I'm sure you're all aware, last night the Facebook campaign page of Pastor Floyd Hartsell posted a couple of photos of myself and one of my staff, who is sitting with me now. Along with these photos was a post that asked its readers to speculate on the nature of the relationship between myself and this staff member. Although the writer of the post was careful not to say it in so many words, the implication was that I'm gay." He lifted his head high. "I'm here this morning to tell you all that this is indeed the case. I *am* gay."

Cameras flashed and loud murmurs rebounded around the room almost instantly, but Sam held up his hands and once more the audience fell silent.

"It was never my intention to hide my sexual orientation. I simply felt that to reveal it would detract from what I was trying to do here in North Carolina. However, the writer of the post alluded to both the nature of my relationship and my support of the SCOTUS decision, so I felt the time had come to set the record straight—no pun intended."

Another ripple of laughter made its way through the audience.

"Ladies and gentlemen, I'd like to introduce you to Mr. Gary Mason." He paused. "My fiancé."

TO hear the way Sam's words were greeted, Gary could've been forgiven for thinking Sam had just announced the Second Coming.

From his position on the sideline, Curtis smiled encouragingly, and Sam gave Josh a nod.

Josh stepped forward. "The senator will now take questions."

A man on the front row raised his hand and was acknowledged. "Chris Mendell, *News & Observer*. Senator, was this engagement a knee-jerk reaction to Pastor Hartsell's post?"

Sam gave a rich, confident laugh. "Certainly not. Gary and I have been together for a year. We met in Raleigh, where Gary resides. And the engagement took place over Christmas." He glanced at Gary fondly.

"Let's just say Gary got a surprise when he reached the bottom of his Christmas stocking."

Laughter greeted his words. Sam's demeanor was amazing. He came across as confident and self-assured, and if Gary hadn't known the truth, he would have been completely taken in by the performance.

"And how about you, Mr. Mason?" Chris asked. "How do you feel about this whole situation?"

"I was shocked, of course, to see our photo on the Internet, but once I got over that, I was kind of relieved too." He flashed Sam a quick smile. "It hasn't been easy keeping our relationship quiet, so having it all out in the open is a relief."

"Why did you keep it a secret?" another journalist asked.

"Because if we'd announced it, there might have been some factions in the state who'd say we were doing it for the publicity," Sam said in a firm voice. "We didn't want that. We didn't want anything to deflect attention away from the reelection campaign. That is more important than what is going on in our private lives. And that brings us to another point: our privacy. Our relationship is nobody's business but ours. I know that as a public figure, I live in the spotlight, but this had nothing to do with my public life." With another glance to Gary, Sam smiled. "All anyone needs to know now is that we're a committed couple who plan to marry when the elections are over."

Gary met his gaze. He knew it was an act, albeit an amazing one, but the light in Sam's eyes at that moment, the way his face glowed, was truly beautiful.

"What pained us both about last night's post on Facebook was that it… demeaned our relationship," Sam said. He spoke quietly, but his voice carried throughout the hushed room. "We weren't doing anything wrong. We're simply a couple planning our wedding, and that post made us look... sordid, I suppose is as good a word as any. When we saw that, we both decided it was time to step out of the closet, as it were. Neither of us wants to hide anymore."

A barrage of questions broke out, but they washed over Gary's head. His attention was focused on Sam.

When at last the questions petered out, Josh took control once more. "If that's all, ladies and gentlemen?"

Someone at the back piped up. "One last question?" The speaker rose to his feet. "You know what would be really great right now?" He grinned. "If the senator and Mr. Mason shared a kiss for the cameras."

Loud chatter and bursts of applause followed his words.

The reporter gazed around at his fellow members of the press, nodding and grinning at them. "Right? We wanna see the happy couple in a lip-lock. What do you say, Senator?"

Gary's heart pounded. No *way* was he ready to go that far.

Sam cleared his throat. "I'm sure you do," he remarked dryly, which caused a few chuckles. "However, it's not really appropriate for a press conference, and I'm sure many of us here will agree with that. This is not a daytime soap opera."

Murmurs of approval echoed his statement, and the reporter's face fell.

Josh coughed. "Thank you for attending, ladies and gentlemen. Copies of the senator's statement are available as you leave the offices. All that remains is to thank Senator Dalton and Mr. Mason for talking so candidly with us about what is a private matter."

There were nods as Sam and Gary stood to leave, along with calls of "Congratulations, Senator!" They exited the room, Curtis leading the way, and headed up the staircase to Sam's office.

Once inside, Gary sank into a chair, fighting to breathe evenly. "God, I was so nervous just then."

Sam patted him on the shoulder. "You did great."

Curtis murmured in agreement.

"I know, that last one threw me too. I hadn't expected it."

Josh came into the office and closed the door behind him. "Fucking Barry Donovan," he said, clearly seething. When Gary frowned, Josh gestured with his thumb toward the door. "That dickwad who asked you two to kiss. He's one of Hartsell's supporters, and you can bet he asked that to try to embarrass you." He smiled at Sam. "And you reacted like a true statesman." Josh gave Gary a kindly smile too. "You were great, Gary. A natural."

"Oh, I wouldn't go that far," Gary said with a chuckle. "I'm just glad you'd covered the table fully with that white cloth so they didn't get to see my knees shaking."

Becky, Curtis, and Josh laughed.

Sam didn't, however. "You gave a performance to be proud of," he said softly.

The warmth of his praise made Gary's insides all fluttery.

"It didn't surprise me that there were a couple of negative questions," Josh said.

"But what can you expect when you invite journalists who write for a Republican-owned newspaper?" Curtis retorted.

Josh sighed. "Like I could refuse them entry. Freedom of the press and all that, right?"

Gary stared at them. "There were negative questions?"

Curtis laughed. "I don't suppose you followed everything that closely—you were probably too busy trying to stop your knees from knocking."

A phone rang in Becky's office, and she scooted in to answer it. A moment later she stuck her head around the door. "Sam, line one, now."

"Is it someone I can call back later?" he asked, pulling a face.

Becky shook her head. "I wouldn't if I were you. It's your mom."

Gary watched all the color drain from Sam's face.

He sat down heavily. "Damn it, I *knew* I'd forgotten something." He placed his hand on the phone and paused. "Guys? A little privacy, please?"

Everyone nodded and got up to leave. Once outside the office, Curtis shook his head. "Moira is going to be pissed. I wouldn't like to be in Sam's shoes right now." When Gary gave him a quizzical look, Curtis grinned. "Wait till you meet her. That is one scary woman." He patted Gary on the arm. "You have all that to come."

Gary stared after him as he and Josh disappeared into Josh's office. *Oh my.*

Chapter Five

Telling Mom

SAM picked up the phone with no small amount of trepidation. "Hi, Mom."

There was a moment of silence. "Do you want to explain why I had to watch a televised press conference to learn about my son's sexual orientation and his engagement?" He caught the quiet huff of displeasure. "Of course, I'm just your mother."

Damn it. There'd been so many things to think about that morning—getting engaged to a stranger was enough to make *any* man forget to call his mom—that it had completely slipped his mind. "Yeah, about that...."

Mom chuckled. "It wasn't as big a shock as you might imagine. Well, the part about you being gay certainly wasn't."

What the fuck? "Excuse me?"

"Oh, sweetheart. Seriously? You're thirty-three and not once have you brought a girl home to meet your parents."

"Did you ever stop to think that might be because I have very scary parents?"

There was an infinitesimal pause before she continued. "I considered it, yes, but then I dismissed it. Who would be scared of your father and me?"

Sam coughed. "Anyone who's ever met you?"

"Don't change the subject," she said abruptly. "Just tell me how you've been dating this... Gary for a year and we're only hearing about him now. What's wrong with him?"

"Nothing's wrong with him!"

"Well, there has to be some reason why you haven't brought him to meet us," she commented dryly. "He's not an ax murderer, is he?"

He didn't even dignify that with a reply.

"Well, if he's not a murderer, I can't see what could be so horrible about him that you wouldn't want to—" There was a heavy pause. "Oh my God—he's a *Republican*."

"No, Mom, he's not. He works in my campaign office, remember?" Sam explained patiently.

"He looks perfectly normal. At least from what I could see. Cute too."

"Mom!" he groaned.

"What? Can't I say he looks cute? But he does!" She snickered. "You're just worried that I'll ditch your father and turn into a—what's that word again? Oh yes—cougar."

She did not just say that. "Since when do you know about cougars?"

Mom cackled. "Sam, I'm fifty-eight. I'm not dead." A pause.

Oh Lord, what next?

"Another thing. You stayed with us over the holidays. As far as I can remember—and granted, my memory isn't what it used to be—I don't recall seeing you unwrap a fiancé that you managed to find under the Christmas tree."

Aw, crap. "Look, it's a long story."

"Then I look forward to hearing it. Over lunch. This Sunday. *Both* of you." Another pause. "Right, Sam?"

"Yes, Mom." Like there was any point in arguing with her. She always won.

"Excellent. I'll expect you both on Sunday. Lunch will be at one as usual, so don't be late, please. And Sam?"

"Yes, Mom?"

"It was a good press conference. And I hope that post bites Hartsell in the ass." With that last stunning remark, she disconnected.

Sam stared at the phone. His mom never failed to amaze him.

Gary peered around the door at him. "Am I okay to come in?"

"Sure."

He entered and sat in the chair facing Sam. "Is everything okay?"

Sam laughed. "Sort of. You and I get to have lunch with my parents this Sunday."

Gary's brow wrinkled and he bit his lip.

"What's up?" Sam asked.

"Curtis was talking about your mom, and…."

That explained a lot. "Did he say something to make you nervous?"

"Maybe?"

"Well, right now whether she likes or doesn't like you is immaterial. We have a bigger problem. She watched the press conference on TV and wants to know when I found time to get engaged, seeing as I spent the holidays with them."

"Oopsie."

Sam stared. "Did you just say what I think you said?"

Gary flushed. "It was something my mom used to say. I guess I picked it up from her."

"Used to?" It struck Sam that he knew so little about Gary.

"Yeah. I lost both my parents when I was thirteen." His smile was so sad. "Do you mind if we don't talk about this right now?"

Silence fell, one that didn't feel entirely comfortable.

"Sure. Absolutely." The last thing Sam wanted was to upset his…. *Damn. I have a fiancé.*

That was going to take some getting used to.

Gary cleared his throat. "Anyway, back to your mom. Are you going to tell her about… this?"

Sam frowned. "I don't know yet." He tilted his head to one side. "What do they say about the odds of keeping a secret being inversely proportional to the square of the number of people who know it?"

Gary chuckled. "Not sure if that can be proven, but it sounds reasonable enough. You're thinking if you tell them, the odds are greater on someone finding out you just told the press a whopper?"

Sam nodded. "I think I need to come up with something else to tell my parents. I don't think they should know about our… agreement." Though what he was going to say, he had no idea.

"Josh says when you're ready, he'd like to go through a few things he's setting up for this week."

Sam got up and walked around to Gary's side of the desk. "About that. I think it might be a good idea if you go home, collect what you need, and come back here. We can travel to my house this evening in my car. Unless you want to follow me in yours?"

"Mine's in the shop right now. I get a ride from one of the guys who works the phones."

"No problem," Sam said with a smile. "I'll take you home to pick up what you need and then we'll go to my house."

He stared at Sam. "This evening?"

Sam chuckled. "You heard Josh. We're both taking some time off. And what you said earlier was true. We need to spend at least a few days getting to know each other. Especially if we're going to face my parents in five days' time. My mom misses nothing."

Gary sighed. "Great. More pressure. Just what I need."

Sam gazed at him for a moment before patting his arm. "This is what you signed up for, after all. Now let's go see what my whirling dervish of a PR man has cooked up for us this week." He waited until Gary was standing before fixing him with a firm stare. "You are still sure you want to do this? That remark about pressure doesn't sound too positive."

Gary gave him a half smile. "I think I'm still on edge after that press conference, that's all. When that last reporter asked us to kiss, I wasn't sure which way it was going to go."

Sam huffed. "Don't you worry about him. Right now we have much more important things to do—like talk to Josh, for one thing." He opened the door. "Shall we?"

Gary gave a single nod and led the way out of the office, and Sam followed him.

It felt like they were about to step onto a rollercoaster, one whose peaks and valleys lay hidden from view.

Sam hated not being able to see where things were heading.

"YOU rent a place in Raleigh during the campaign, don't you?" Gary gazed at the sights of downtown Raleigh as they sped through in Sam's Explorer.

Sam nodded. "Although I warn you now, it's not what you might be expecting."

"Oh, now you've intrigued me." He imagined Sam staying in a modern house, maybe three bedrooms, a front yard with trees....

"If you knew where I lived in Asheville, my choice of rental property wouldn't seem all that strange." He turned the car left at the Crabtree Valley Mall, and the scenery greened up a whole lot, but when Sam turned right onto Ebenezer Church Road, Gary had no clue where they were headed. When Sam eventually pulled the car off the road onto a wooded lot right at the edge of Umstead Park, Gary's jaw dropped.

"It's a log cabin." A redwood log cabin, nestled in the middle of woodland, with a wraparound deck. "Does it have hot and cold running water?"

Sam snickered. "Rustic-looking, isn't it? And yes, ye of little faith, it has all the necessary modern amenities." He cleared his throat. "Okay, the floor in the main living space is *very* rustic because it's reclaimed barn wood, but the fireplace works and there's plenty of space."

"How many bedrooms?" Because judging from what Gary could see, the cabin didn't look big enough to have more than one. He had visions of sharing Sam's bed for however long they were going to be staying there. Not that he disliked that particular idea. Not at all.

"Two bedrooms, one bath, and a total of 1,200 square feet," Sam said. He stopped the car in the little parking lot next to the cabin and switched off the engine. "I like the fact that it's close to civilization while giving the impression of being on the outer edge of it. There's a local store for groceries, which is great. And it's fairly quiet around here at night. Not as quiet as in Asheville, but it will do."

They got out of the car and went around to the trunk to collect Gary's bag. He couldn't take his eyes off the property. "I bet you haven't got cable," he said at last.

Sam laughed. "You'd lose that bet." He unlocked the front door and led Gary inside.

Gary gazed up at the sloping wooden ceiling. It had obviously been one large open space at one time, but partition walls had been constructed across one end of the building. "How many rooms in total?"

"Four. This is the main family room."

To the left was the fireplace with its stone surround, while to the right was the kitchen area, with a huge stove, plus a microwave, enormous refrigerator, washer and....

"It has a dishwasher!" Gary exclaimed.

Sam laughed. "Didn't I say all modern amenities?" He walked past Gary toward the walled-off rooms, beckoning him to follow. "This is the bathroom, and beyond here are the bedrooms. Yours is the one after mine." He gestured to the door. "Drop your bag and coat there, and then we'll get dinner started."

Gary did as instructed, then followed Sam back into the main room.

"Is there anything you don't eat?" Sam asked him, peering into the refrigerator and pulling out a package.

"Nothing that I can think of. I'm not that keen on cabbage, but I can eat it if I have to."

Sam's eyes sparkled. "I'm not about to force feed it to you, not when I have steak in here." He tilted his head. "Does steak do it for you?"

"Every time," Gary replied with a smile. "Love my meat."

`Sam broke out into a fit of coughing. "Okay... I'll get dinner started...." He paused. "I've got a bottle of red wine, if you'd like a glass."

Gary nodded. "Yes, please."

Sam uncorked the bottle and poured out two glasses.

Gary peered at the wine label. "I like merlot." He clinked his glass against Sam's. "Here's to unconventional beginnings." He grinned.

Sam laughed. "Yeah, that sounds about right. Unconventional beginnings." He snorted. "About as unconventional as they come." He put down his glass. "Baked potatoes and green beans good with these?"

"Sure, sounds good."

Sam pointed to a stool near the black granite-topped counter. "Sit there. It won't take long to get dinner ready, but while I'm doing that, can you pull up your e-mails? See if Josh has sent us the details for this week yet." He switched on the oven and then handed Gary a small card that had been tucked into the corner of a cork noticeboard on the wall next to the refrigerator. "The code for the Wi-Fi."

Gary nodded and fished out his phone from his pocket. Once he'd changed the settings, he scrolled through until he found Josh's e-mail. "Damn. We're going to be busy. Steven, our photographer, will be at the office tomorrow morning at ten. He's going to be our shadow for the rest of this week."

"Here's a question. Is Steven in on it?"

Gary skimmed through the e-mail. "Apparently not. All Josh has told him is, now that we've officially come out, we're doing catch-up with all the positive publicity." He raised his head to meet Sam's gaze. "So I guess we have to be careful what we say around him, huh?"

Sam nodded as he rubbed olive oil, salt, pepper, and crushed garlic into the steaks. "So what's the plan?"

"Josh wants him to come with us tomorrow afternoon to the SPCA. I've got a two-hour shift that can't be changed."

"How long have you been a volunteer?"

Gary shrugged. "Since I started college, I suppose." He went back to the e-mail. "Thursday Josh has arranged interviews in Raleigh."

Sam stopped, his fingers shining with olive oil. "How many interviews?"

"Four. The first is with *Out*."

"*Out* magazine?" Sam's eyes widened. "Wow. Josh doesn't pull any punches. We'd better have our stories straight for that one." He smirked. "Pun intended. Who else?"

"*The Advocate*, *HuffPost Politics*, and *Slate*."

Sam snorted. "We'd better be on the ball for those." He pursed his lips. "I didn't think *Slate* would have been all that interested. They're not particularly gay-focused." Sam gave a shrug. "They're liberal, though. Will Steven be with us for all the interviews too?"

"Yes, clicking away with his camera. Thursday night we'd better drive to your house in Asheville, because Josh wants Steven to take photos of us at your place the following morning and that afternoon in the Biltmore Village. Saturday Steven's coming with us to the Biltmore Estate. He wants to take pictures of us walking through the gardens and looking at the house, as if we're checking it out as a possible venue for the wedding." Gary had to smile. "Josh thinks of everything, doesn't he?"

"From every angle," Sam added. He left the steaks to rest while he scrubbed a couple of potatoes before drying them, rubbing salt into their skins, and placing them on a baking sheet in the oven.

Gary's stomach clenched. The thought of all those interviews and photo ops was a daunting one.

"What else?" Sam wasn't looking all that thrilled with the prospect either.

Why would he—his life has just been turned upside down too.

"That's as far as this week goes, but Josh says Steven is putting together a list of places he wants us to visit after that."

"He is *not* coming with us on Sunday, all right?" Sam said firmly. "We'll have enough coping with my parents without adding a photographer to the mix." He reached into a deep drawer and pulled out a griddle pan.

Gary picked up his glass and took a drink. It was going to be a long couple of days.

DINNER was over, the dishwasher was running, and they were sitting in front of the fireplace, where a fire burned brightly, the logs hissing and crackling. They sat on the bigger of the two couches that faced the window, the sky black beyond the glass.

Gary had his legs curled up under him, his feet bare. Not for the first time, Sam noticed what a good-looking man he was. He was slim, with short blond hair, although it was longer on top and Gary kept brushing it away from his eyes.

Sam peered at Gary's feet next to him on the seat cushion. *What is it about bare feet that I find so sexy?* He'd been fighting the urge to ask if Gary wanted a foot massage ever since he'd kicked off his shoes and pulled off those cute little socks.

Then it occurred to him that they were wasting time. This was the perfect chance to get to know each other a little better before they'd be on show with Steven. Sam wasn't sure where to begin, until he recalled their conversation after his phone call with his mom.

"Earlier today you mentioned your parents." Sam couldn't help noticing how Gary stiffened instantly. "I'm sorry, but I thought maybe it was something I needed to know."

Gary took a sip of wine and stared into the fire, its flames casting a warm glow on his face. There was a look of such sadness that Sam's chest constricted.

"Forget I asked," he said quickly. "I shouldn't have—"

Gary held up a hand to silence him. "But you *should* have. God, we announced to the press today that we're getting married. *That* means yes, you should have." He took another drink, but a longer one this time. "Where I grew up, our house was a stone's throw from the Pisgah National Forest, and I loved it there. My friends and I did BMX biking on the mountain bike trails that were seconds from my doorstep."

Sam said nothing, but studied Gary's tight face. He had no idea where this was leading, but he figured it was best to keep quiet until Gary was done.

"So, one day when I was thirteen, I was out with my friends on my bike. It was cold—it was December, after all—but I was in my warm jacket, speeding along the trails that crisscrossed through the forest. We were on those trails as soon as it was light enough, I recall. Well, to cut a long story short, there was this one point where two trails that ran parallel to each other, swerved to converge and then crossed. It was always exciting when we got there, like it was a race to see who got to cross first."

Sam winced. "Uh-oh. Sounds like a recipe for an accident."

"And it was. I collided with another rider, got flung into a tree, and broke my wrist and my right leg."

"Ouch."

Gary nodded. "You can say that again. What made it worse was that my parents and I were about to go on vacation. For the first time ever, we were going away for the holidays. Except as soon as I got injured, Mom started talking about canceling." He scowled. "I couldn't let them do that. They'd worked really hard to afford the vacation in the first place. And secondly I'd have been miserable if they'd stayed at home and missed out on an exotic vacation because of my stupid biking."

"What did you do?"

"Called Uncle Tim, Mom's brother, and asked him to talk some sense into them. They took some persuading, I'll tell you, but eventually they agreed that I'd stay with Uncle Tim while they went to Sumatra."

Sam widened his eyes. "Sumatra? Very exotic indeed." Gary didn't smile, however, and a horrible suspicion began to form in Sam's mind. He did the math and didn't like what he came up with. "December, you said…. December *when*, exactly?"

Gary's eyes caught the firelight. "2004," he said simply.

Aw, fuck. "The tsunami," Sam whispered, aghast. "Were… were their bodies ever recovered?"

Gary nodded. "It took a while, of course, for all the bodies to be identified, but yeah, my uncle was able to bring them home." He quickly took another swallow of wine.

Sam's heart went out to him. To lose both parents at that age had to have been terrible. "So who brought you up?"

"My uncle. No grandparents on either side, so there was only him."

Sam studied Gary's expression. "Do you get along with him?"

Gary did a seesaw motion with his hand. "He was older than my mom and didn't have any kids. There was just the two of us. We managed to get by, I suppose, but by the time I left for college, I guess I was relieved. It just felt like it had been a legal arrangement and nothing more. We keep in touch. I get a card on my birthday and at Christmas." His face tightened even more. "And he always calls when it's the anniversary of their death."

"Which has just passed," Sam said as that realization hit him.

Gary nodded. "The holidays tend to pass me by. Maybe that will change as I get older."

Sam fell silent. He couldn't begin to comprehend what Gary had gone through. Then he recalled something Gary had said that morning. *Was it only this morning when he agreed to all this?* It felt longer than that. For one thing, Sam felt like he'd known Gary for longer than two days. "You said your debts had been a weight. Didn't your parents have life insurance?"

Gary sighed. "As far as I can make out, they took out a policy when they got married, but when they died, it only paid out enough for the funerals and part of the money needed to... bring them home. So I've always had to work my way through college—hence the debts."

Sam tentatively stretched out his hand and covered Gary's on the seat next to him. "I am so, so sorry your start in life was so traumatic. But if you think about it, breaking bones like that saved your life. Otherwise you'd have been there too."

Gary looked him in the eye. "There have been times when that's crossed my mind. But more often than not, I've hated the fact that I lived and they didn't." He swallowed. "I still miss them."

"Of course you do," Sam said earnestly. "That's only natural."

"Yeah, but sometimes I find it difficult to recall exactly what they looked like. That's why I don't think I'll ever grow tired of saying 'oopsie.'" He smiled. "It's like a tiny bit of my mom is still with me."

What a sweet thought.

Sam glanced at the clock over the fireplace and sighed. "Pleasant though this is, we'd better get to bed.

We need our beauty sleep if we're going to look gorgeous for the camera tomorrow." He batted his lashes.

Gary laughed, and the joyful sound eased a little of the tension in him. "Yeah, some of us need more sleep than others."

Sam gaped. "Excuse me?" he said indignantly.

Gary's eyes widened. "Not you," he squealed. "Me! Why would *you* need more sleep, you're gorge—" He bit off the words before they escaped.

Sam tried not to smile, but *damn*, it was an effort. He cleared his throat. "And on that note…." He got up off the couch to tend to the fire, his back turned toward Gary to hide his grin.

He thinks I'm gorgeous. Good to know.

"I'll say good night, then," Gary said, his voice cracking.

"Good night. Sleep well."

Sam waited until all was silent and Gary had gone to his room before drawing in a shuddering breath. *My fiancé is a very sexy man.* Too bad theirs was an engagement—and marriage—of convenience. He pictured Gary's face in his mind, the haunting beauty that had been so obvious when he'd spoken about his parents.

Damn. I could so easily fall for that face.

What he was discovering was that what lay on the inside was just as beautiful.

Chapter Six

Wednesday

CURTIS came into Sam's office. "You got a minute?" His gaze flicked to Gary, sitting next to Sam. "Oh, good morning, Gary," he said absently before giving Sam his full attention.

Sam sighed. "I thought I wasn't here to work. We're meeting the photographer, Steven, this morning."

"Yeah, well, you'll want to see this." Curtis handed Sam his phone. "Hartsell issued a statement five minutes ago, as a reaction to your press conference yesterday."

Lord, was it only yesterday?

Beside him, Gary groaned.

Sam peered at the screen and quickly read the short statement. He gave a snort. "He's just saving face, that's all. He knows we made him look bad."

"What does he say?" Gary asked.

Sam read aloud from the screen. "'How nice it was to see Senator Samuel Dalton finally come clean about his sexuality yesterday in a press conference. It is always refreshing when a politician resorts to honesty, even if the senator had needed a prod to force him out. I still have reservations, however, as to his suitability to represent his Christian constituents. Of course, the senator's private life is his own, and we would not dream of telling him how he should conduct it.'"

Gary scowled. "That remark about Sam not representing his Christian constituents…."

"I told you," Sam said patiently. "He's just saving face in front of his voters."

"Then you need to think again," Curtis said quietly. "That comment was a direct message to all those voters in North Carolina who think of themselves as religious. Have you any idea what percentage of people fall into that category?"

Sam stilled, tension creeping across his back. "No, but I'm sure *you* do."

Curtis nodded. "The percentage for the US is 48.78. Here in NC it's 47.51 percent. I could give you the breakdown of what percentage are Catholic, Baptist, Presbyterian, et cetera, but you don't need to know that. All you need to know is the figure I just gave you. Because that means 47.51 percent of people in this state will be listening to him." When Sam handed him back his phone, Curtis tapped the screen with his finger. "We need to keep a close eye on our friend Pastor Hartsell."

Sam nodded slowly. "Agreed."

A knock at the door had all their heads turning. Josh entered, followed by a tall, thin young man with a large bag slung over one shoulder. "Everyone, this is Steven Pinder. He's the photographer I told you about. Get used to him, because he'll be sticking to you two like glue for a while."

"Anything we need to know about you, Steven?" Sam asked with a smile. "Any bad habits?"

"Maybe we should ask him what his politics are," Curtis said, his manner lighthearted, but Sam knew better.

Steven nodded briskly. "That's actually a fair point." He smiled at Sam. "I voted for you last time, Senator, and it's looking likely that I'll do exactly the same this time, especially after yesterday." When Sam arched his eyebrows, Steven grinned. "That little sh— that pastor had no right outing you like that. And it's about time we had a few more rainbow flags on show around here."

Gary chuckled, and Steven's face flushed.

"God, don't get me wrong. I'm not gay—but my brother is. You should have heard him on the phone to me yesterday." He laughed. "He said, and I quote, 'It's about fucking time.'"

Sam smiled. "Glad to be working with you, Steven." He gestured toward Gary. "My fiancé, Gary Mason."

Gary gave Steven a polite nod.

Steven rubbed his hands together briskly. "Any coffee going around here?"

Curtis snorted. "You're going to fit right in."

"HEY, Gary. We saw the press conference on TV. You kept that quiet!" From behind the SPCA reception desk,

Stella grinned at him. "Talk about a dark horse. Why didn't you tell us you were dating the dishy Senator Dalton?"

"That might have something to do with the fact that I wasn't out," Sam remarked dryly as he came through the door behind Gary.

Stella's eyes widened. "Oh my God." She glared at Gary. "You might have said something," she hissed.

Sam snickered. "No, trust me, it was much more fun this way." He gestured to Steven, who had appeared next to him, camera pack in hand. "This is Steven, who is shadowing us today."

"And we didn't say anything because it's supposed to be business as usual," Gary added.

Stella's eyes sparkled. "Oh, I see. Would you two gentlemen care to sign in, please?"

Sam and Steven approached her desk and signed in the visitors' book.

She thanked them and peered at the clipboard next to her keyboard. "Well, I hope you brought a change of clothing, because you're giving the dogs a bath this morning."

"Really?" Sam grinned. "This might prove highly entertaining."

Gary lifted his eyebrows. "Oh, you think so? Well, I'm glad about that, because you'll be joining me." He winked at Steven. "That's right, isn't it? Josh did say Sam was to get involved?"

"Oh, totally," Steven agreed, his face straight.

"Come on," Gary told the stunned-looking Sam. "This way." He tried not to smirk as he led the two men through the hallways until they reached the rooms where all the animal grooming took place. "There's a wash station here. All the dogs get bathed every one to three months." He smiled at the young woman who was standing by the wash station. "Hi, Stacey. Looks like I'm taking over for you."

Stacey grinned. "Nice timing." She glanced past Gary to where Sam was standing, looking around the facilities. She stared. "Is that…?"

Gary nodded. "I get to have a helper today." He snuck a sideways glance at Sam. "A VIP."

Stacey bit her lip. "Then I might stick around." She removed her long blue apron and handed it to Gary.

"Why?"

She gave him an innocent look. "Oh, no special reason."

Gary began to get a bad feeling. "Who's next on the list?"

That innocent expression didn't alter. "Dinky."

Sam snorted. "Dinky? What is he, a Chihuahua?"

Gary fired him a hard stare. "Hey, don't laugh. It's the little dogs that are the worst when it comes to bath time." He returned his attention to Stacey. "Dinky? Really? He had a bath last week." His stomach churned. This was not good.

"Yeah. I don't know what he's been rolling around in, but God, he stinks." Stacey stepped away from the wash station. "I'll go fetch him." She left the room, her shoulders shaking.

"Why is she laughing?" Sam whispered.

"You'll know soon enough," Gary said. He put the apron over his head and reached into the drawer of a nearby cabinet to find another. "Here, put this on." He glanced over at Steven. "And I recommend you take any photos from over there. You wouldn't want to get your camera wet."

Steven stared. "From over here?" He did as instructed, however, removing his camera from its bag and peering through the viewfinder.

"He's out here," Stacey called from the connecting room.

"Why didn't she bring him in?" Sam asked as they stepped toward the other room.

Gary snorted. "Probably because he didn't want to come in here."

Sam laughed. "Didn't want to? What kind of a— dear *Lord*!"

Dinky lay on his belly, paws stretched out in front of him. All two hundred pounds of black, glossy-haired Newfoundland. He raised his muzzle slowly and eyed Gary with what could only be described as mistrust.

Sam chuckled. "*Dinky*? Who were they kidding?"

"One thing you need to know about Dinky," Gary said in a low voice.

"And what's that?"

"He is the most uncooperative, ornery, frustrating dog when it comes to baths." He spoke out of the corner of his mouth. "Whatever you do—show no fear."

BEFORE Sam could react, Gary slowly took a step toward the sprawled dog. "Hey, boy. Come on."

Dinky took one look at him, chuffed, and lowered his muzzle onto his paws.

"Aw, come on, Dinks. You know we gotta do this, right?" Gary said in a coaxing tone.

Dinky closed his eyes, and Gary crept closer. The dog opened one eye and let out a low, menacing growl, baring his teeth.

Sam had an uneasy feeling about this. "He's never bitten you, right?"

"He's tried," Gary replied darkly. He took one more step toward Dinky, and the dog got up and scooted under the table. He just about fit. "Aw, Dinks. Why'd you have to go and do that?" He met Sam's gaze. "Okay, now I need your help."

"What do you want me to do?" Sam asked, conscious of Steven's camera clicking away.

"Sneak up from behind, sort of a pincer movement," Gary said. "You need to drive him to me. I'll grab him, and we'll drag him into the bathroom."

"We?" Sam was trying not to laugh. "It'll take two of us?"

Gary glared. "Do you *see* the size of him?"

Sam made his way carefully around the table, watching Dinky's reactions. The dog apparently couldn't decide which of them was the greater threat. His head swiveled from Sam to Gary and back to Sam again. "Moving in—now!" He darted forward, arms wide, and Dinky scrabbled out from under the table across the tiled floor—right into Gary's arms.

"I got him!" Gary shouted in triumph.

"He's not in there yet!" Stacey yelled, smirking.

Dinky had other ideas. He wriggled and writhed, trying to worm his way out of Gary's grasp, but Gary held on valiantly, in spite of the hair that got up his nose. Dinky managed to squirm out of his arms and turn around, but Gary grabbed him again, getting a face full of Dinky's butt for his trouble. Sam dove across to help him, only to end up with two heavy front paws on his chest, pushing him away. Between them they dragged the struggling dog toward the bathroom, Dinky scrabbling with his paws, trying to grab hold of anything reachable. When they reached the doorway, Dinky dragged his claws across the doorjamb, holding on for dear life.

"Damn. This dog really does not want a bath!" Sam exclaimed.

"What have I been saying?" Gary groaned, trying to pry Dinky's claws from the woodwork. "He was like this last time too." He glared at Sam. "For God's sake, help me stop him from holding on to the doorframe! He's making my arms ache."

Sam caught Dinky's paws. "Okay, Dinky, time to let go of the door." From behind him he caught Stacey's muffled laughter. Steven was laughing too, and Sam scowled at him. "I think I want to get these photos before Josh gets to see them," he said decisively, doing his best to unhook Dinky's paws gently. When he finally achieved that, he helped Gary drag Dinky to the opening in the wash station. Dinky squirmed once more, wriggling as they tried to maneuver him toward the other end where the sprayer was located. Once he got there, however, he stopped.

"What the hell?" Sam stared as Dinky stood next to the sprayer, as docile as could be.

Gary burst out laughing. "Yeah, this is normal too. Once he gets in here, he's all, 'okay, spa me.' I swear, he's schizophrenic. Watch this." He stroked Dinky's head. "Okay, boy, stand still."

Dinky obeyed instantly.

"Now we get him wet before we apply the shampoo." Gary reached for the sprayer and dampened Dinky's long hair. He took the bottle of dog shampoo and squirted it liberally over the pelt. Gary grinned at Sam. "Well, don't just stand there. Help me rub it all in."

Sam leaned over, and between them they worked the shampoo into a rich lather. Dinky appeared totally relaxed.

Stacey smiled. "I think you two have everything under control. I'll leave you to it." She gave Gary a nod. "See you around, Gary. Nice to meet you, Senator Dalton. I hope we get to see you here again." She left the room.

Gary looked around. "Hey, where are the towels?" he called after her.

"In their usual place," she yelled back.

Gary groaned. "Aw, shit."

"What's up?" Sam asked, rubbing Dinky's back, the dog just standing there, peaceful as could be. Sam shook his head. "I don't get it. I thought you said he was uncooperative when it came to baths."

Gary laughed. "He just hates getting *in* the goddamn bath. Once he's in there, he loves being pampered. Don't you, boy?"

Dinky lifted his muzzle and let out a soft wuff.

"This isn't so bad," Sam said, cleaning behind Dinky's ears. From behind them came the sound of Steven's camera clicking away.

Gary snickered. "I hate to tell you this, but you see how much Dinky likes the water?"

"Uh-huh."

"Well, when it's time to get him out of it, let's just say he's not that keen on the idea." He picked up the sprayer and began to wash away all the soap, leaving one very wet, even heavier dog, his hair clinging to his body. Gary put the sprayer aside and gave Dinky a firm stare. "Okay, Dink, don't give me a hard time, all right?"

Dinky chuffed.

Gary headed toward the door, and Sam stared at him. "Where are you going?"

"To fetch the towels that Stacey conveniently left in the other room." He met Sam's gaze. "Whatever you do, don't let him out of there."

GARY left the room, smiling. He liked Sam's manner with Dinky.

You can tell a lot about a man by how he acts around animals. So far, Sam was doing just fine.

"Hey, Dinky, where'd you think you're—"

Loud shouts and squeals followed from the bathroom.

Gary hurried back into the room to see Dinky standing in the middle of the floor, tongue hanging out, looking for all the world like he was grinning. Sam was soaking wet beside him, as was Steven, although he was farther away.

Gary sighed. "You let him out of the tub, didn't you?"

"Let him? As if I could stop him. He weighs more than I do! And once he saw you leaving, he apparently wanted to follow." Sam laughed. "Look at the state of me. I already had a shower this morning. And all he did was shake himself off."

Gary joined him, kneeling beside him while they rubbed Dinky down with the towels. The contrary animal stood there and let them. Gary caught Sam's gaze. "That *was* you squealing like a girl just now?"

Sam glared. "That never happened, okay?"

Behind them, Steven guffawed. "Too late, Senator. I'm a witness too."

Sam shook his head. "No such thing as loyalty anymore." He rubbed Dinky's head. "How long has

Dinky been here?" The dog lifted his muzzle and licked Sam's chin, and Sam laughed. "Why, thank you, Dinky."

"Three months now. They're hoping someone will adopt him, but I suppose his size puts a lot of people off." Gary scooched Dinky under his chin. "How could anyone not love a big old hound like you, hmm?"

"How did he come here in the first place?" Sam asked.

"He was found chained to a railing by the side of the highway. Apparently his owners had had enough of him." Gary scowled. "How anyone could treat an animal like that is beyond my comprehension." He glanced at Steven before turning to Sam and speaking in a low tone. "I don't suppose you've thought of getting a dog?" He couldn't keep that hopeful note out of his voice. "Dinky really likes you. I can tell."

Sam stroked Dinky's head. "It's a nice idea, but right now? It's just not practical. I'm only home on the weekends while the campaign is going on. The rest of the time, I'm in Raleigh in the cabin, which stipulates cats or small dogs in the lease. It wouldn't be fair to have a dog under those circumstances."

Dinky suddenly leaned against Sam, and Gary's heart did a little flip-flop. The man was adorable.

Sam smiled at the dog. "Yeah, I like you too. Maybe if you're still around after March…." He glanced at Gary. "But I suppose that's unlikely."

Gary sighed. "I don't really know." He lifted his chin and gazed at Steven. "You got plenty of pictures?"

Steven nodded, grinning. "Josh is gonna love these. And by the time he's finished, every animal lover in North Carolina is gonna love you two."

Sam's stomach rumbled loudly and he flushed. "Is it dinner time yet?"

Gary laughed. "No, it certainly is not. My shift has only just started. Next we clean the cat boxes. Then we take the dogs for their walks." He gave Sam a grin. "You'll get your dinner when you've earned it, Senator."

"Slave driver," Sam mumbled under his breath, but he was smiling, so Gary wasn't too concerned.

"So, do you like cats?" he asked quietly while they were taking off their aprons.

"I like them. Unfortunately, my body doesn't." When Gary gave him a quizzical glance, Sam shrugged. "I have an allergy to kitty fur. So maybe I should sit this one out?"

Gary snickered. "Just this once. But *you're* walking Dinky, okay?"

Yeah, Sam's wide-eyed stare was just plain adorable.

"YOU ready to eat now?" Gary asked Sam as they returned the dogs to their cages.

Dinky jumped up and placed those heavy paws on Sam's shoulders. Gary had expected an instant reply, based on Sam's noisy stomach earlier, but Sam was too wrapped up in Dinky to respond.

Gotta love a man who loves dogs.

Sam ruffled Dinky's hair. "You're a good boy, aren't you? And you didn't pull my arms out of my sockets once."

Dinky rewarded him with a huge lick on his cheek.

Sam gave him a last pet and then closed the cage door on him, and Dinky was up against the mesh instantly, letting out a cute whine.

"I think you have yourself a new friend there," Gary said softly.

Sam crouched next to the cage and curled his fingers through the holes in the mesh. Steven was there immediately, copying his crouch to get a good camera angle. What Gary really liked? Sam wasn't doing it to provide Steven with a photo op; he was simply saying good-bye to Dinky.

When he was done, Steven stowed away the camera. "Okay, guys, I'll see you in the morning at the campaign offices. We can meet there before we head off to the first interview. Make sure you look dazzling, all right? I'm going to go back to my studio and send these photos to Josh. Be prepared to see yourselves everywhere, boys!" He grinned and left them by the cages.

Gary tried not to laugh when Sam regarded him with the biggest puppy-dog eyes he'd ever seen. "*Now* can we go have dinner?"

The more time Gary spent around Senator Sam Dalton, the more he liked what he saw.

Chapter Seven

Thursday night

"WOW." Gary stared through the windshield as they left downtown Asheville behind them and turned off 70 onto 694. "You really do live out in the boonies, don't you?"

Sam laughed. "I wouldn't necessarily describe Chunn's Cove as the boonies. It's quiet and peaceful, and yes, it is a wooded area, but I have Asheville right on my doorstep. Other things, too, like the Blue Ridge Parkway. You ever spend time there?"

Gary shook his head. "Where I grew up, there was a forest just beyond our back fence, remember? That was where I used to spend a lot of time when I was a kid. Once I got into my teens, I didn't get out much. I always wanted to go there, though. The pictures I've seen of it look so pretty." He chuckled. "I've never been to the Biltmore Estate either."

Sam gave a mock gasp. "And you grew up around here? Shocking." He indicated right. "This is our turnoff." He swung the car onto Vance Gap Road, and instantly Gary could see the difference. The sun had set an hour before, and already it was difficult to discern what lay ahead. There was no street lighting and before them was nothing but trees, but every now and then a driveway snaked off the road and the lights of houses could be glimpsed, hidden in the foliage.

"How long have you lived here?" Gary peered ahead, wondering which house would turn out to be Sam's.

"About four years. To be honest the house is probably too big for just me, but I love it." He pulled the car off the road into a driveway, and soon he was parking in front of what looked like a single-story wooden house. The site sloped down to the right where Gary could see a double garage.

"I'm guessing you don't have many problems with neighbors," he said with a chuckle. From where they were, he couldn't even see another house.

"It's on a two-and-a-half-acre lot," Sam said, "so yeah, it's fairly private. And don't let the first view fool you. The house is built on top of a slope, so what you're seeing is the top floor." He switched off the engine. "Come on in and I'll give you the fifty-cent tour."

They got out of the car, and once they'd retrieved their bags and coats from the trunk, Sam locked it and they crunched their way across gravel to the front door. Sam let him in, and Gary stepped into the house.

"It's pretty much open plan on this level," Sam said, leading him into a wide area where Gary saw a kitchen and dining room, around the corner from a living room. "There's another living room on the floor below, along with two of the three bedrooms. I figure the larger of the two could be yours. That way you'd have your own space whenever you're here. There are two couches down there and a wide-screen TV too. We'd share the kitchen, but there's plenty of cabinet space."

Gary nodded, although the idea of sitting alone watching TV while Sam was on his own on the floor above struck him as a lonely way to live.

"I like having breakfast out there on the deck," Sam said, pointing to the sliding doors beyond the dining area. "There are three decks at the back of the house, all of them looking out at the mountains and trees. There's a deck outside what will be your living room too." He smiled. "I'll show you to your room."

Gary followed him through the house and down a flight of stairs. He liked the room Sam indicated: it was big enough, with its own bath, and the idea of being able to step out onto the deck in the morning was a pleasant one. He peered through the adjoining door into the bathroom before checking out the closet. "This is nice."

Sam beamed. "I'm glad you approve. So how about you leave your bag here and we can go up to the kitchen to make some dinner?"

Gary nodded. He left his bag on the chair next to the bed and followed Sam upstairs. "I don't suppose you have another bottle of wine hiding around here somewhere?" he asked hopefully.

Sam laughed and reached up to a wine rack next to the refrigerator. "Was today that bad?" He pulled out a bottle of red wine and uncorked it.

Gary groaned. "Not for you, obviously, but then you're used to being interviewed, photographed, poked and prodded...."

Sam halted in midaction. "Did it feel like that?"

There was a moment of silence before Gary responded. "I'm probably exaggerating. It was just so strange to have all those questions fired at me, like my opinion was worth something."

Sam poured him a glass of wine and placed it on the countertop in front of him. "Of course your opinion is worth something. Those people really wanted to know about you, what you thought about the SCOTUS decision, how it feels to be suddenly thrust into the spotlight...."

"It feels uncomfortable, that's how it feels," Gary said softly. "But you know what? I've only had to put up with this since Monday night. You've had this for years." He tilted his head. "How do you do it?"

Sam leaned on the counter and looked him in the eye. "By taking it one day at a time. But even I have my moments when it all gets to be too much. Would you believe me if I said I'm getting really tired of having a shadow? And we've only had him with us for two lousy days." He sighed. "Don't get me wrong, I like Steven, but I'm growing less and less happy about the idea of having photos of us everywhere I look. You know, I keep hearing that damn camera of his clicking even when he's not there?" Sam chuckled. "Now that's bad."

"We have two more days of this," Gary reminded him.

Sam lifted his own glass. "Then here's to a Steven-free evening."

"I'll drink to that." They clinked glasses, and Gary took a drink of the mellow wine. "So, what's on the menu for tonight?"

Sam flushed. "I'm sorry, but it's late, and I really can't be bothered to cook, so… what do you say to pizza? There's a pepperoni and mushroom one in the freezer."

Gary grinned. "You and I are really going to get along."

Sam raised his glass one more time. "I will definitely drink to that."

"OKAY, just one more."

Sam groaned. "Steven, you said that half an hour ago. You've taken shots of us in the kitchen, making lunch. Making bread, of all things." Gary snickered and Sam glared. "Hush, you. I'll deal with you later."

Gary turned his face away, but not before Sam caught sight of that evil grin.

He turned back to Steven. "You've had us in the backyard, raking leaves. On the couch, curled up watching TV. Having lunch."

Steven pouted. "Yeah, but you won't do the one I *really* want."

Beside him, Gary snickered once more, and Sam narrowed his gaze before returning his attention to Steven. "No, no, and no. We are *not* letting you take pictures of us in bed."

"Aw, come *on*. Two good-looking guys with nothing but a white sheet covering your… assets? I know a few magazines and websites that would love photos like those." His eyes gleamed. "Why not?"

"Josh will kick your ass, that's why not. He wants this to come across as a sweet, wholesome relationship, remember?" Sam scrolled through his contacts and then held out his phone. "And if you think I'm wrong, go ahead: call him."

To his surprise, Steven grabbed the phone and made the call. He left them sitting at the dining table while he walked away, muttering quietly into the phone.

Sam shook his head and then remembered Gary's reaction. "And *you* certainly weren't helping matters. You're supposed to be on my side."

Gary chuckled. "I'm sorry. I knew there was no way you'd let him, though. And you're right, of course: it's not the impression Josh wants us to give. Can you imagine Hartsell's reaction if photos of us in bed together went out in the media? Even if they were only in a gay-friendly magazine."

Sam guffawed. "Yeah, like they wouldn't make it onto the Internet in seconds. We'd just be giving him more ammunition. He'd be spouting off about us setting a bad example, indulging in sex before marriage, or something like that."

"Having said that," Gary said slowly, "there is always the possibility that him seeing such photos *might* have a positive result."

Sam stared. "How do you work that out?" His heart pounded. He did *not* want to think about him and Gary in a bed.

Gary bit his lip. "He might take one look at them and spontaneously combust. Job done—one less asshole to worry about."

There was a second or two before both of them burst out laughing.

"We're being evil," Sam said between giggles, relief flooding through him.

"No, just hopeful," Gary suggested, a wicked glint in his eye. Sam was starting to see a whole other side to his fiancé, and he *really* liked what he saw. There was a mischievous streak running through Gary that was only now beginning to emerge. Of course, it had been difficult not to notice when they'd been making bread together and Gary had rubbed a floury hand all over Sam's face. Steven had *loved* it.

Ah yes—the flour….

"Just so you're aware, I'm not going to forget that trick you pulled." He gave as stern a glare as he could manage.

Gary's expression was apologetic. "I'm sorry about that." Then he spoiled it by grinning. "*So* not sorry. The look on your face…."

"Okay, guys." Steven rejoined them, his face crestfallen. "You were right. Josh vetoed the bedroom shots." He handed Sam his phone.

"Told ya," Sam said smugly.

"But he did say I can take more romantic shots, should the situation arise," Steven added with a gleam in his eye.

"Romantic—not sexy," Sam stressed. "Remember, Josh wants these to go out on Twitter, Instagram, Facebook, yeah?"

"All right," Steven grumbled. "You guys are no fun." He glanced at the clock on the kitchen wall. "Okay, ready for the Biltmore Village? I'll just make sure I've packed all my filters for the camera and then I'll meet you at the car." He walked out of the dining area.

Gary leaned in close. "You've visited the Biltmore Village, right?"

Sam nodded.

"Well, is there any place where we might accidentally lose Steven?"

Sam huffed. "I think that counts as wishful thinking." Not that he didn't love the idea too. "Let's try to enjoy it, all right? We can look in all the windows and *ooh* and *ahh* for the camera. Let's just... block him out and concentrate on our surroundings."

"Okay," Gary agreed with a sigh. "But if a situation presents itself?" He grinned. "All bets are off."

Sam shook his head. "You're a bad man, do you know that?"

For a second Gary's grin faltered. "Mom used to look at me and say, "But you were so *sweet* when you were a baby. Someone came in the night and swapped you for a little fiend.'"

On impulse Sam gave him a hug. "I like the sound of your mom." Gary felt good in his arms for those brief seconds, his body warm and firm.

Then it was over and Gary stepped away.

"Come on," Sam sighed. "Let's go look pretty for the camera." He peered at Gary. "And if you promise to behave, I might buy you an ice cream."

Gary snorted. "Wow. I'm underwhelmed." Then he grinned. "Make it a double scoop maple pecan and you got a deal."

They walked to the front door, Sam's arm at Gary's back. "I like you. You're a cheap date."

Gary snickered as Sam locked the door behind them. "I'm lulling you into a false sense of security. Wait till you see what I ask for in a few weeks, when I've gotten to know you a little better."

The first thought to cross Sam's mind took him by surprise.

Spending more time with Gary? Bring it on.

"AW, can't we go in there?" Gary asked, pointing to a children's clothing shop, Just Ducky.

Sam gave him a hard stare. "Just so we're clear on this? There are no ducks in there. It's just a cutesy name, all right?"

Next to him, Steven snickered.

"Really?" Gary's innocent expression wasn't fooling Sam for a second. When Steven fiddled with his camera, Gary leaned closer. "Can we go now?" he whispered. "I mean, the Village is a charming place, really quaint, but when you've seen one window display, you've pretty much seen them all." He snuck a glance at Steven. "And there are only so many photographic variations you can take of two men looking at... stuff."

Sam knew exactly what he meant.

"Hey, guys?" Steven flicked his head toward the hotel behind them. "I need to go find a restroom, okay? Will you two be all right on your own for a sec? I'll be as quick as I can. Then we can take some more pictures at the art gallery."

Gary turned his head and did an eye-roll.

Quick as a flash, Sam nodded. "Sure. We'll wait right here."

Steven grinned and handed them the bag with all his camera equipment. "Take care of this for me?"

"No problem," Sam said smoothly. "Take your time." He waited until Steven was out of sight before grabbing Gary's arm. "Quick." He tugged him away from the hotel and across the cobbled street.

"What are we doing?" Gary asked, his eyes wide.

"Ditching Steven," Sam said with a grin. "You with me?"

Gary's eyes lit up. "You bet."

Sam slung Steven's bag over his shoulder and grasped Gary's hand. "Let's make a run for it, back to the parking lot. We're going to have to move fast."

They sprinted along the street, Gary twisting to look back over his shoulder.

"Any sign of him?" Sam said breathlessly.

"No, but we're too visible." Gary glanced around and tugged Sam toward the corner. "Quick. This way!" Sam surged ahead and Gary laughed. "Hey, wait for me!"

Sam cackled loudly. "Keep up, slowpoke!" He pointed to a playground. "Through there. It's a shortcut to the parking lot."

Gary chuckled, panting. "You *have* been here before. Done this before too?"

Sam snorted. "No, this is all you."

"Me?" The word came out as an adorable squeak. "What have I got to do with this?"

"Getting me into bad habits!" Sam yelled back as they reached the lot where they'd parked the Explorer, Steven's beat-up Jeep next to it. Sam placed the bag in the trunk, swung the car out of the lot, and sped through the quaint streets.

"Hey, wait a minute!" Gary shrieked. "You're heading the wrong way! Isn't this the street the hotel is on? He'll spot us for sure. Turn off!"

"Too late—duck!" Sam cried out as he caught sight of Steven standing on a street corner, looking up and down, scowling.

Gary promptly bent over, and Sam did his best to turn his face away, still chuckling. "Do you think he saw us?" Gary whispered.

Sam cackled once more. "Why are you whispering? And you can get up now."

Gary sat upright and peered in the rearview mirror. "He'll have seen the car. He knows what you drive."

"Yeah, but he still has to catch us."

"Where are we going?" Gary asked, laughing. "Or have you not thought that far ahead?"

"The last place Steven would think of looking for us," Sam said. "We're going to the Biltmore Estate."

"Aren't we supposed to be going there tomorrow?"

Sam nodded, grinning. "Which is why he'll never think of looking for us there," he explained patiently.

"You're a genius."

"See, *now* you're getting to know me!"

THEY were sitting on a wrought-iron bench, with a back that resembled a pattern of fern leaves, in the Biltmore Conservatory. Behind them, rising high into the air and bracketed by tree ferns, was a huge camellia shrub, its flowers deep red. Gary was feeling at peace for the first time that week.

His body was peaceful, at least. The same couldn't be said for his mind.

Sam was quiet beside him, watching the visitors walking around the Conservatory, apparently drinking in the scents and the sights. Three hours of strolling around the grounds—heaven. It was ironic that they'd ditched Steven. The place was perfect for just the kind of romantic photos Josh was after.

We'll make it up to him. We'll come back another day.

Gary could see why Josh had spoken about using the Biltmore Estate as a possible venue for the wedding. The mansion resembled a French chateau, and its gardens were magnificent.

And suddenly there he was, at the heart of what had been gnawing at his thoughts ever since Curtis's e-mail had arrived that morning. He'd shoved it aside each time it had surfaced, but Gary couldn't leave it any longer.

"Can we talk?"

Sam inclined his head toward him. "Sure. Is anything wrong?"

That was it. Gary wasn't sure.

"I got an e-mail this morning," he began. When Sam didn't react, he pressed on. "From Curtis. It was the first draft of our agreement."

That got a reaction.

"Oh." Sam let out a sigh. "I wondered if you'd want to discuss it."

Gary twisted on the bench so he faced Sam. "This marriage…." He tried his best to form his thoughts into coherent sentences. "Everything isn't as cut-and-dried as it appeared on Tuesday, is it?"

"Go on," Sam said quietly.

"Well, at the press conference, you told the reporters we were planning our wedding."

"That's right."

Gary was nodding. "Yeah, but in this contract Curtis sent me, it doesn't state that we're definitely getting married. It simply states that a wedding might take place in the future. And I figured you had to know about this." He cocked his head to one side. "So you're okay with us getting engaged, but as far as getting married is concerned, that's up in the air?" He held up his hands. "Don't get me wrong. I'm not saying 'why isn't this etched in stone?' I'm just trying to find out exactly where I stand. Because this isn't where I thought I was standing a couple of days ago."

Sam's face fell. "Look, it's just…." He swallowed. "I asked Curtis to allow for the possibility that the wedding might take place because… there's part of me that still feels this is wrong. Getting engaged is one thing—engagements are broken off all the time. But marriage? That's different. We'd be making vows to each other, supposedly in the sight of God, and—"

"You didn't like the idea of lying?"

Sam sighed heavily. "It would be real enough on paper, but in here?" He tapped his temple and over his heart. "It wouldn't be a real marriage in here, no matter what I kept telling myself." He bowed his head. "We'd be living a lie, and I don't think I can agree to that."

"Aren't we living a lie now?" Gary suggested. "It's not a real engagement, is it?"

Sam said nothing.

"So what's the plan?" Gary's head was buzzing.

"We stay engaged for a while, we see how the election goes—we play it by ear." He lifted his chin and met Gary's gaze. "This is how I'm feeling now. Things might change. *I* might change. Who knows if I'll feel the same way in a month, or two months…?"

Gary stared at him. "I don't know what to say," he said simply.

"I never meant to jerk you around," Sam said. "But things moved so freaking fast on Tuesday, and before I had time to turn around, I found myself engaged. I guess when I'd had time to think, I panicked and called Curtis."

Gary took a deep breath. "I think what hurts most about all this is that you didn't think you could mention it to me. You let me read it in an e-mail. I know we haven't known each other long, but I really thought we were getting along."

"We *are*," Sam stressed. "Like I said, this is just how I'm feeling now. A month from now we could be announcing a date for the wedding." He reached across and laid his hand over Gary's. "Are you happy for us to continue? Knowing what you know now?"

Gary stared at Sam's hand, his mind turning Sam's words over and over. "Can you make me a promise?"

"That depends," Sam said, a note of caution in his voice.

"Don't shut me out. If it's something that affects our agreement, let me know." He turned his hand palm upward, and Sam laced their fingers. It was an unexpectedly intimate gesture.

"I promise." Those deep brown eyes were focused on him. "I... I've really enjoyed spending these last few days with you. I don't want to spoil that friendship. Because we are going to need to be friends if this is going to work."

Gary nodded. "Okay, then."

Sam smiled and withdrew his hand. "You think we'd better go home and face the music? That's where Steven will probably be waiting for us." He pulled out his phone and grimaced. "Oh Lord. There must be at least fifteen texts on here from him and Josh. We'd definitely better go."

"Yeah, sure."

Gary rose and walked with Sam toward the exit. He knew why that e-mail had hurt. It had nothing to do with Sam not being the one to break it to him and *everything* to do with the fact that Gary's hopes had been quashed.

He wouldn't have minded being Sam's husband. Not for a second.

Chapter Eight

Saturday

"MORE coffee?" Sam held up the pot.

Gary nodded. "Thanks. Any word from Josh yet?" He glanced at his phone on the table. "I thought we'd have heard from him before now."

Sam had a bad feeling about that. There'd been no Steven awaiting them when they'd gotten back to the house the previous evening, which had been a relief. But they'd spent the night waiting for Sam's phone to ring. When no call or more texts had materialized, Sam had heaved a sigh of relief, and he'd gone to bed with a lighter heart.

Not that he'd slept much when he'd gotten there. He couldn't get the conversation with Gary out of his head. What surprised him was Gary's attitude. Sam had expected him to be relieved that the wedding wasn't a done deal, but that wasn't how it had come across. It was almost as if Gary had been… upset.

I'm probably reading too much into this. The contract just took him by surprise, that's all. Curtis had agreed to the cautious wording of the agreement once Sam had explained his reasons. *Let me get used to the idea of being engaged. I don't want to rush into anything.*

He gazed across the table to where Gary was drinking coffee and staring out at the view. "It is beautiful here, isn't it?"

Gary smiled. "That it is." He cocked his head. "Listen to those birds. What a gorgeous noise. They sound so happy, like they're glad to be alive."

Sam chuckled. "Yeah, more like we had a rain shower during the night, and right now all the birds can spot the worms."

"Cynic." Gary drank some more. "I prefer my interpretation." Sam's phone chirruped, and he raised his eyebrows. "I guess we know who that will be."

Sam sighed and peered at the screen. "No guessing required." He connected and put the phone to his ear. "Good morning." He kept his tone light.

"Put me on speaker," Josh demanded instantly.

No *Good morning, boss*. No nothing. *Fuck.* They were in trouble.

Sam did as instructed and placed the phone on the table between them. "Okay, we can both hear you."

"Did you boys enjoy your little stunt yesterday?"

Gary stiffened and narrowed his lips. Sam could understand that reaction. Something in Josh's tone put Sam's back up too.

"I still employ you, don't I?" he inquired. "I was just wondering, because the way you're speaking to me right now is—"

"That's right, you pay me to do a job," Josh ground out. "So yeah, I'm allowed to be pissed when you go and screw up my plans. Especially when they're already starting to pay off."

"What are you talking about?"

Josh huffed. "I don't expect you to follow yourself on social media, because heaven knows you've got better things to do right now, and besides, that's what you hired *me* for. But those pictures Steven took at the SPCA the other morning? You should see how many impressions they've earned us. Even the ones from the village yesterday are getting liked and retweeted already. And as for that video he shot of you two bathing Dinky? Unbelievable reaction."

"Wait—what video?" Gary straightened in his chair, staring at the phone.

Josh snickered. "The one I told him to shoot. The one that's in the top twenty of YouTube's most viewed list already. Everyone loves it."

"You told Steven? How about telling us?" Sam demanded. He'd had no clue about the filming.

"I figured you'd be more natural if you didn't know," Josh said airily. "And it worked!" A pause followed. "So let's all agree that Josh knows what he's talking about, and do what I tell you, all right? Steven will be there any minute. You're all going to the Biltmore Estate, where you are going to do *exactly* as he tells you and make both him *and* me happy. You both got that?"

"Fine." Sam was fuming. He knew Josh was good at his job, but it really rankled to hear that tone from him.

"Good. I'll expect to see some stunning photos later, then. Bye for now." Josh disconnected.

Sam expelled a long breath and counted silently to ten.

"I think we just got our wrists slapped," Gary murmured, reaching for the coffee pot.

Sam gave a loud snort. "Ya think? Here, don't drink all the coffee. Save some for me. I think I'm going to need it."

"Where does he get off talking to you like that?" Gary looked as pissed as Josh had sounded. "I mean, I know he's working hard to put a positive spin on things and reverse some of the damage done by Hartsell's post, but honestly?" He let out a low growl. "When someone pushes me too hard, I tend to push back." He locked eyes with Sam. "For future reference."

Sam couldn't hold back his smirk. "Thanks for telling me. I'll be sure to stay on your good side."

It took a second or two, but eventually Gary relaxed and chuckled, and the tension out on the deck eased a little.

"And if it helps? I'm with you on this."

Gary smiled. "Good to know. I think we both need to lighten up a bit before Steven gets here." He fished his phone out of his pockets and grinned. "Hey, I've got a text. It's from Dinky. *'Are you bringing that nice man back to see me? And when is he going to adopt me? My bags are all packed.'*" He grinned.

Sam laughed. "Thanks. I needed that." He caught a different sound on the morning breeze. "I hear a car. Steven must be here." He was trying to work up some enthusiasm for the day, but so far it just wasn't happening.

"Can I drive today?" Gary asked suddenly.

That stopped him for a moment. "Sure, but it's not that far to the estate, so you won't have much driving to do." A thought crossed his mind. "And I'll bet you anything you like that it won't be as pleasant as yesterday, when it was just the two of us."

Gary's expression softened. "Yeah, no takers on that one." He rose. "I'll go get ready. Steven will want to take a lot of photos to make up for yesterday." He picked up his mug and the now-empty coffee pot and went into the house.

Sam lingered on the deck, drinking in the morning sunlight and the sounds and scents of the outdoors.

The loud rap on the door plunged him back into the present.

He went through the house and let Steven in.

Steven strode into the hallway, his lips pursed. "I suppose you two thought it was funny, running off like a pair of six-year-olds."

And there was Sam's bad mood back to stomp his ass. He'd been prepared to be apologetic, but Steven's attitude was pissing him off right from the get go.

Fuck it.

"Yes, we did, actually." He beamed. "Ready for today?"

Steven arched his eyebrows. "That depends on you two. I'll just have to insist that if I have to visit the restroom, you're both coming with me." When Sam snickered, he coughed. "Yeah, I didn't mean that how it came out."

Gary came up from his room, a jacket slung over his shoulder. The dark green T-shirt that clung to his torso matched his eyes perfectly. And those jeans....

Lord, he has a nice ass. Nice everything, as far as Sam was concerned.

"And here's the other bad boy. You gonna behave today?"

Gary's jaw set. "Of course." He turned to Sam. "Are we ready to go?"

Sam nodded. "I just have to put the dishes in the dishwasher. Then we can leave."

"Can I have the car keys?" When Sam gave him an inquiring glance, Gary shrugged. "Just wanted to set up my phone to get us there, seeing as I've never driven there before."

Sam opened his mouth to speak, but Gary flashed him a warning glance. He came across to Sam and held out his hand for the keys. When Sam placed them in his palm, Gary leaned closer, and his lips brushed against Sam's cheek. Sam's heart pounded at the unexpected gesture, until Gary whispered, "Keep him talking, okay?" He pulled back and winked before walking past Steven with a polite smile and exiting the house.

Sam bit back a smile. *What the hell is he up to?*

"So, what did you two get up to after you dumped me?" Steven asked.

"We drove around for a while and came back here," Sam said with a nonchalant air.

"Oh, I get it. That explains a lot. Booty call, huh?" Steven leered. "What is it with gay men? I swear, my brother acts like he's in heat all the time. He gets more bedroom action than I do." Steven shook his head. "I'm obviously batting for the wrong team."

For some reason his assumption about Sam's sex life hit a nerve.

"Not that it's any of your business, but not all gay men are alike. And *some* of us think some things are worth waiting for." It was close to the bone, but Sam didn't want Steven thinking they were a pair of sluts.

From what he knew so far about Gary, that description didn't fit him at all.

Steven paled. "I'm sorry. I shouldn't make unnecessary assumptions. And you're right, it's none of my business." He swallowed. "For the record? I think it makes a refreshing change."

"It's not something I'm comfortable talking about," Sam said quietly. That much was true.

"Gotcha." Steven cleared his throat. "Shall we go?"

Sam nodded. He grabbed his jacket and they left the house.

"I'll follow you guys," Steven told him, and walked toward his Jeep.

Gary was beckoning Sam excitedly. "Come on, quick!" he gritted out before climbing behind the wheel.

Sam jogged across and got into the passenger seat. "What's the hurry?" he asked, securing his seatbelt.

Gary switched on the engine, and the car lurched into life. He spun the wheel and headed up the driveway at top speed.

Sam looked back toward the house. "Er, why aren't you waiting for Steven to follow us?"

Gary snorted. "Trust me, Steven isn't going to be following us far today." He pulled out onto Vance Gap Road and headed south on 694.

Sam stared at him. "And why is that?"

Gary gave a little shrug. "Because I let the air out of his tires." He grinned. "All of them."

Sam was seriously impressed. "Your mom was right, you know that? You *are* a little fiend." He couldn't stop smiling.

Gary gave a gasp. "Ouch, that hurts. I was nice. I left him a foot pump so he could reinflate them."

"Where did you get a foot pump?"

"I found it in your trunk," Gary said, and Sam started laughing. "What's so funny about that?"

"That's the pump I use for blowing up the basketball Curtis and I play hoops with now and again."

"Oopsie." Gary gave him an adorably sheepish grin. "Might take him a little longer than I'd thought, then."

Sam shook his head. "You're incorrigible. And there was you telling Steven you were going to behave."

"I *am* behaving!" Gary insisted. When Sam gave him an inquisitive glance, he grinned. "I never said I'd behave *well*, did I?"

Sam snorted and gazed through the windshield. "Want to tell me where we're going?"

"Someplace I've never been," Gary said. "And I wanted it to be just us." He glanced across at Sam. "That okay with you?"

"Perfectly okay." He relaxed into the seat. "You do know Josh is going to kick both our asses for this, right?"

There was that grin again. "I have a plan. Trust me."

It came as something of a shock when Sam realized he already did. Then a thought occurred to him. "Gary? Let's turn off the phones?"

"MY God, this is amazing." Gary's hushed tone was full of awe. "It's still winter, and yet look at it. It's so beautiful."

Sam had to agree.

They stood in an overlook parking lot, gazing out over hills and valleys dotted with trees, a vast, majestic expanse of sky above them. The dark hills rippled across the landscape, against the sky that was a startling shade of blue. The mountains farther off rose up out of the mist, their peaks sharp.

"I love the Blue Ridge Parkway." Sam had many fond memories of summers hiking through those mountains with his parents, of standing at the foot of majestic falls and watching the water cascade powerfully over rocks. They'd walk alongside a creek and stop to eat a packed lunch before walking some more. "I want you to see Bald Mountain. It's awesome, the way it rises up from a canopy of green, its sides so smooth."

He was dimly aware of Gary nodding beside him. "It's sights like this that make you believe in a Creator," Gary said quietly. "All this beauty, as far as the eye can see. Every turn of that road coming here brought something else to look at. Blink and you missed it." He turned to Sam. "Thank you."

"You brought us here, remember?" Sam said with a smile.

"Yes, but that was only because you spoke so fondly of it. I wanted to see it for myself." He drew in a deep breath. "I could stand here for hours, drinking it all in."

Behind them, the bushes rustled. They turned to look, and Gary caught his breath at the sight of a raccoon, standing on a fallen tree trunk, watching them, its heart visibly pounding. "Hey there, little guy," he whispered.

Sam smiled. "I'd say take a picture, but he'd probably run for it before you got your phone ready."

"I can try." Slowly Gary raised his phone and held it out. "Aren't you a handsome fella?"

The raccoon let out a cute, high-pitched squeal and stood up on its hind legs.

Sam laughed softly. "Oh, you're a bold one, aren't you?" Next to him, he caught the soft click as Gary took his photo. "See? He posed for you."

The raccoon gave another squeal and disappeared back into the trees.

"That's what you sounded like the other day," Gary said. "You know, when Dinky splashed you." His eyes sparkled.

"*Splashed* me? It took ages for my clothes to dry out after that." He was about to say more, but one look at Gary's smirk told him to remain silent. *Someone* was having fun with him.

Ping.

"And there's another one," Gary said with a sigh. "He's going to keep messaging us until we answer him, you know that, right?"

Sam glared at his phone, his screen full of texts from Josh. "I only turned it on to take pictures."

"Then tell Josh my plan and he might leave us in peace," Gary reasoned.

He had a point.

Josh answered after one ring. "Where are you?"

"The Blue Ridge Parkway," Sam said. "Look, I'm sorry, we just—"

"Save it," Josh said shortly. "I'm only trying to save your ass after Hartsell outed you, that's all. Only trying to win you more voters. Only—"

"Josh!"

Silence. "What?" He sounded like a sullen, petulant kid.

"We are taking selfies all over the place here. For you. And Gary took photos yesterday at the Biltmore Estate, which is where we were. Selfies too. We will e-mail you everything." He paused. "Will that make you happy?" The whole situation was ridiculous, but he didn't want to piss Josh off any more than he had to. The guy was worth his weight in polls.

"Yeah, it just might." Josh sighed. "Sorry, boss, but I'm doing my best here for you."

"I know you are, and I had no right to mess up your plans like this. But you know you said Gary and I needed to spend time together?"

"Uh-huh?"

"It's not so easy getting to know someone when there's always someone else there." He let Josh digest that.

The silence that followed his words said a lot. "Gotcha. Go be with Gary. I'll see you on Monday. And Sam?"

"Hmm?"

"Good luck tomorrow." Josh disconnected.

It took a moment for his meaning to filter through Sam's brain. *Tomorrow? Tomo—Aw, crap. Lunch with Mom and Dad.* He'd actually forgotten.

"Ready to move on?" Gary asked.

Sam smiled. "Sure. And I know just where I want us to go next."

Chapter Nine

Peace and Bliss

THIS is such a beautiful spot," Gary murmured, gazing at the creek, the water so still it was a perfect mirror, reflecting the trees above their heads. They sat on top of a pile of rocks, only reached by crossing the creek on stepping-stones. Gary had his knees drawn up, his arms wrapped around them. Sam sat next to him, his face turned up toward the sun.

"You should see it on a less calm day," Sam said, "when the water cascades over the rocks into swirling pools. I've sat here for hours, watching fish darting in and out of the undergrowth, the water so clear you could see everything. Fall is the best time to be here, though. The colors of the leaves are just stunning."

"It's pretty stunning now," Gary assured him. "Is this somewhere you used to come with your family?" He could almost picture Sam as a little boy, running along the water's edge, laughing, his face alight. Right then he exuded calm.

Sam nodded and regarded the scenery. "My granddad used to bring me here during the summer, when Mom and Dad were busy with the store. We'd spend hours out here." He chuckled. "Of course, not everyone had a cell phone back then, so my granddad frequently got in trouble for bringing me back late." There was a faraway look in his eyes. "We just lost track of time."

"Is he still living?" Gary asked. He found himself wanting to know more about the man sitting beside him. There was something about Sam that drew him, something that made him eminently… likable. *Maybe that's why he appeals to so many people.* Sam gave off the impression of being a decent, honest man—a good trait in a politician—but it wasn't just a surface thing.

Gary thought back to their conversation about the contract. Once he'd gotten past his own feelings, what had emerged was genuine admiration. Sam had honor, integrity—all things Gary didn't see enough of in the world of politics. And even though what they were doing felt contrary to those very traits, in another sense it felt strangely right.

That was why he didn't follow the constant barrage of election news. Working the phones was one thing—he found it easy to talk to people, and he liked what Sam stood for—but that was as far as it went. As far as Gary was concerned, it was generally easy to spot when a politician was lying: their lips moved.

Only, Sam isn't like that. Gary had to smile to himself. Senator Samuel Dalton—was he really the one good apple in a barrel full of unripe, worm-eaten ones? *Or maybe it's more the case that I'm projecting onto him. I'm allowing my attraction to him to cloud my judgment.*

Because Gary was definitely attracted to the gorgeous senator. And it wasn't just for the way he looked either.

"We lost Granddad a year ago." Sam's voice was hushed. "He was eighty-three. I know everyone wishes they'd had more time when someone they love dies, but I was glad he went when he did. He'd suffered from severe arthritis for a good few years, and I wanted him free of pain. Of course, he hadn't been the same since Grandma died." His smile was sad. "We figured he just wanted to be with her."

One look at that sweet expression and all Gary wanted to do was enfold Sam in a hug. He told himself that would be okay—they were *engaged*, for God's sake—but something held him back. Maybe the knowledge that Sam was right. This wasn't real.

"Is it just you? No brothers or sisters?"

"Just me."

A comfortable silence fell, and Gary was content to sit and drink in the tranquil scene. Birdsong rippled through the air, and a light breeze stirred the surface of the water. Just then from above their heads came a burst of song. Gary craned his neck to see a cardinal perched on a branch overhanging the creek, its song a long note followed by ten short chirrups. It was such a happy sound that he couldn't help smiling. More birdsong followed, only this time he couldn't tell its source.

"Finch," Sam said quietly. When Gary glanced at him, Sam shrugged. "My granddad used to point out all the birds when we came here. You grow accustomed to their songs."

Gary leaned back, his arms supporting him. "Can I get something clear before we meet your mom tomorrow?"

Sam peered at him. "You're not getting nervous, are you? I told you to forget what Curtis said. He was just trying to get a rise out of you."

"It's not that, it's just...." He sat up, hugging his knees once more. "I sort of got the impression from your reaction to her calling you that she didn't know you're gay."

Sam fell silent, but the birds more than made up for it, singing their little heads off. After a moment, Sam nodded. "You're right. She didn't know. Neither of them did."

"Whoa. Hell of a way to learn, then—watching it on TV." The hair lifted on the back of his neck. "They... they're not... I mean, they're okay with it, right?"

Sam laughed. "Trust me, if my parents were homophobic, I wouldn't be taking you anywhere near them." He paused, then gave a sigh that tugged at Gary's heart. "The thing is, when I'm not involved in election campaigns or engaged in senatorial activities, I run a hardware store."

Gary thought he might had read that somewhere. "Where?"

"In Asheville. My great-grandfather started it, and then Granddad took over. My dad grew up working with him, and eventually he took it over. The store's a damn sight bigger than when Great-Granddad Walter first built it, but it's nowhere near as big as those multinationals that pop up all over the place. It's still a family-run store. Dad retired a couple of years ago, and I took over."

"I guess I should ask: who's minding the store right now?"

Sam smiled. "Dad. He always steps in when I have state business to attend to." He snickered. "But boy, does he gripe about it. Lucky I know he loves doing it, right?" Sam swiped a hand through his short hair. "Anywho, my parents would talk about when I'd give them grandkids, and wouldn't it be a hoot if I only produced daughters, and hopefully one of my kids would want to carry on the tradition...."

Gary's heart went out to him. "You were afraid you'd disappoint them if they found out the family line ended with you."

Sam nodded, and Gary patted his leg.

"Er, excuse me? Can we say 'adoption'? Surrogacy?"

Sam expelled a long breath. "I know. That was just part of it, though. There was this huge ball of fear in my belly, one that said everything else I was would be forgotten once people knew. I'd just be gay." He stared into the creek, his shoulders hunched over.

Gary sighed. "Look at me, Sam." He waited until Sam had slowly raised his chin and those troubled brown eyes met his. "There are so many things I could tell you about myself—my experiences, my dreams, my fears.... All of them go to make up Gary Mason." He laid his hand over Sam's. "Being gay accounts for just one of them, and it isn't what defines me."

"When you came out, did people look at you differently?"

Gary rolled a shoulder. "Sure. Some did."

Sam nodded. "See, that is what I was afraid of. That people would change the way they view me.

That they'd start analyzing my every move, maybe start acting differently toward me." He swallowed. "I thought maybe my parents would think they didn't know me anymore."

"But you're still you," Gary said softly. "The fundamental things about you haven't changed. You're just deciding to show them a part of yourself they haven't seen before."

Sam stared at him for a moment and then nodded. "I like that."

"Look, there are bound to be a few assholes out there who will have a problem with your sexuality. That's to be expected. Life is not all rainbows and unicorns, okay?"

Sam gasped. "It isn't? Why didn't anyone ever tell me that?"

Gary whacked him on the arm and Sam growled.

"Hey, that hurt."

"Then stop being an asshole and let me enjoy this place before we have to leave it." Gary gazed around him. "This is a really romantic spot," he murmured.

"Do you think so?"

Gary turned to look at him. "Don't you?"

Sam gave a half smile. "I don't have much experience in the romance department."

Something stirred in the recesses of Gary's mind. "About that. We mentioned this briefly on Tuesday, didn't we? I told you I'd had a couple of boyfriends, but that there'd been no one for a year."

"I remember."

Gary waited, but nothing else was forthcoming. "What about you? I know you said you haven't had much time for romance lately, but I was wondering…. What about before you became a senator?"

Sam leaned away, crossing, then uncrossing those long legs that were stretched out in front of him.

Shit. His unease was palpable.

Gary backpedaled. "I'm sorry if I've made you uncomfortable again. It just seemed to me that we should know these kind of things about each other, especially if I'm meeting your parents tomorrow."

Sam stared at him for a moment and then sighed, his shoulders sagging. "That's a fair point." He gazed at the creek. "I've never had a boyfriend."

"Really?" When Sam jerked his head up, eyebrows lifted, Gary gave a shrug. "The strange thing is, I'm surprised to hear that, and yet when I think about it, it's not surprising at all."

"What do you mean?"

"Well, yeah, it's surprising that someone as attractive as you hasn't had a boyfriend, but then again, if you'd *had* one, I guess we'd have known about him by now."

Sam nodded. "Exactly. This is why I didn't date."

Gary snorted. "In that case you've been very fortunate to hook up with some extremely discreet guys. That, or you paid them a fortune to keep quiet." He grinned, but one look at Sam's face made him stop. Sam's expression had tightened, and he swallowed. On impulse Gary reached out and placed a hand on Sam's shoulder. "Sam? What is it?"

Sam remained silent, avoiding Gary's gaze.

Gary thought quickly. It didn't surprise him that Sam might be an intensely private man—he was a politician, after all—and Gary clearly didn't know him well enough yet to be able to judge if his question had really embarrassed the hell out of him or if there was some other reason for his reticence.

When the idea occurred to him, he dismissed it. *Surely not.* There was no way that Sam….

Oh hell.

"Sam, can I ask you something kinda personal?"

Sam turned to face him, brows scrunched together. Then his face cleared, leaving an expression of resignation. "Sure."

"Have… have you ever… been with a guy?" It sounded less blunt than coming right out and asking him if he'd ever had sex. Then it occurred to him that maybe Sam had experimented. "Or with a woman?" he added quickly.

Something flickered in those deep brown eyes, but Sam said nothing.

Holy fuck. "You haven't been with anybody?"

Sam lowered his gaze, and shock ricocheted through Gary. The thought that no one had ever held this beautiful man, had ever known what it was to hold him in their arms….

Gary couldn't stop himself.

He reached across and gently lifted Sam's chin with his fingers. Sam looked into his eyes, and Gary's chest constricted. "Sam… may I give you a kiss?" His heart hammered and a shiver ran down his spine.

Sam's breathing quickened. "I'd like that."

Gary shifted closer until he could feel Sam's breath on his face. Slowly, so slowly, he closed the gap between them, and their lips met in a soft kiss, mouths closed, the feel of those warm lips intensifying the tremor that rippled through him. When he drew back, Sam was staring at him, his eyes wide.

"Can I ask you a question?" Sam's words were so faint, Gary just about missed them. He nodded, and

Sam cupped Gary's face with a gentle hand. "Can I have another?"

Gary smiled. "You bet." He closed his eyes and let Sam guide their lips together, as chaste a kiss as before, but still one he felt all the way through his body.

When they parted, Sam let out a sigh. "I've waited a long time for that."

"I hope it was worth it," Gary said quietly.

Sam hadn't relinquished hold of Gary's cheek. "Totally." He lowered his hand, and impulsively Gary shifted position until he was leaning against him, his head on Sam's shoulder. After a few seconds, Sam put his arm around him.

Gary had no idea how long they sat like that. He was lost in the moment, conscious of Sam so close to him, that strong arm holding him, the smell of him, warm and comforting. Sam's body had lost its tension, and Gary thought he could sit like that until the sun went down.

"You know what we should do right now?" Sam murmured. "Take a selfie."

Gary snickered. "Aw. Josh will love you for it." He felt Sam's chuckle vibrate through him.

Sam pulled out his phone and held it at arm's length. "Stay just like that." He took the photo and was about to put the phone away when Gary stopped him.

"One more," he said softly. "But this one is just for us. Think you can take a pic at the same time as kissing me?" He wanted to feel that mouth on his one more time.

Sam grinned. "That's what timers were invented for."

Before Gary could say a word, Sam was kissing him, lips pressed together. It was soft, it was sweet, it was chaste....

It was perfect.

They parted and Sam grimaced. "Going to have to move soon. My ass has gone to sleep."

Gary laughed. "We can't have that." Then Sam's stomach gave an almighty rumble, and Gary arched his eyebrows. "Never mind your ass. I think we'd better get some food into you." Reluctantly he got up, extended a hand to Sam, and pulled him to his feet. "Let's go home."

Gary took one last look at their surroundings, trying to fix it all in his mind. He didn't want to forget this moment.

SITTING in Sam's Explorer, staring through the windshield at the two-story wooden house, those idyllic moments of the previous day seemed a lifetime ago.

"I'm not sure I'm ready for this," Gary muttered.

Sam patted his leg. "You'll be fine. Just remember to look her in the eye." He tilted his head and grinned. "And you did remember the garlic and the wooden stake, right?"

Gary blinked.

Sam burst out laughing. "She's not that bad."

Gary fixed him with a hard stare. "I'm sorry, but I'm finding it difficult to take this situation lightly."

Just like that, Sam's mood changed. "Hey, what's wrong?" He spoke softly, his voice reminiscent of the Sam who'd sat next to him on that rock.

"This… this is important," Gary stressed. "If we can convince your parents that we're a couple, we can convince anyone." It had been the only thing he'd thought about all night. He'd loved the day they'd shared, but once he'd gotten that thought into his head, the bubble had well and truly burst.

This was reality.

"Just be yourself," Sam said, his gaze focused on Gary's face. "If she starts asking awkward questions, I'll deflect her, all right? But I promise you, it won't be that bad. And she's sworn she'll be on her best behavior." He smirked. "Which isn't saying much."

"Not helping," Gary growled.

Sam chuckled. "I was trying to make you laugh." Then his eyes widened. "Damn. I nearly forgot." He reached into the breast pocket of his shirt and pulled out a gold band. "This was my granddad's. He left it to me."

Gary stared at it, confused. He sought refuge in humor. "Senator Dalton. My, this is so sudden."

Sam guffawed. "Yeah, she's going to love you." He held up the ring. "What did I say in that press conference? Something about you finding a surprise in your Christmas stocking?"

Gary's mouth fell open. "Shit."

"Exactly. My mom remembers *everything*."

Gary winced. "Whoa. It must have sucked to be you growing up."

"You have no idea." He took Gary's left hand. "This is probably not going to fit, but here goes…." The only finger it fit on was his middle finger. Sam shrugged. "Better than nothing. It's slightly too big for your ring finger, but there's always the possibility that if you wear it on that one, it could fall off. When she remarks on it—and she *will*—I'll come up with a plausible excuse. And try not to lose it. It's just for today, anyway." He smiled and gave Gary a quick peck on the lips. "Now let's get in there before she sends out the Marines to find us."

Gary stilled him with a gentle hand to his arm. "Does it get easier?" When Sam gave him an inquiring look, Gary smiled. "Being more… physical with me. Like that little peck just now."

Sam flushed. "The funny thing is, I did that without thinking. It just felt… right."

Slowly Gary leaned closer. "That's because it *was* right," he whispered. He didn't wait for Sam's reaction, but brushed his lips against Sam's, the movement light and fleeting. When he sat back, Sam's eyes were wide. Gary smiled. "Okay, I promise not to do that in front of your parents, but if they're going to believe this is real, there has to be some… connection between us. Agreed?"

Sam nodded. "Agreed. Do you remember all the things we discussed?"

Gary squeezed his arm. "I've learned my script, Senator. I won't let you down." Then he forgot to breathe when Sam's hand was on his cheek and Sam was kissing him, lips together.

What is it about a chaste kiss from him that makes my heart pound?

Sam released him and sat back. "Time to face the music."

Gary nodded, trying to regain his composure. "Ready as I'll ever be."

Once he'd collected the flowers from the backseat, they got out of the Explorer, locked it, and walked side by side up the driveway to the front door. When they reached it, Gary felt Sam's hand on his back at his waist. "Remember to smile, nod, compliment her on the delicious grilled chicken…."

"Just so long as the chicken is the only thing getting grilled," Gary muttered under his breath. Whatever else he'd meant to say died in his throat as the door opened and a small woman in a plain blue dress and white pearls stood there, smiling.

"You must be Gary. Come on in." She gave a nod toward Sam. "Hi, Son. Good to see you."

Gary stepped past her into the hallway. "Good afternoon, Mrs. Dalton." He held out the bouquet of flowers. "These are for you."

Her smile widened. "Why, thank you. How thoughtful. It's so nice to finally meet you. You'll have to forgive me, but until this week, I had no idea you even existed." She glared at Sam. "But then again, why would I? It's not like I'm important or anything. I'm just your mother."

Sam groaned. "Mom, you promised to be good."

"This is me being good," she said sweetly before fixing Gary with a firm stare. "Do you know, he claims he's never brought you to meet us because we're scary. I'm not scary, am I?"

"No, ma'am." The words came out as a squeak, much to Gary's embarrassment.

"See?" She turned to Sam with a triumphant air before patting Gary's arm. "Now, you come along with me. I have so many questions I want to ask you." She steered him along the hallway, and Gary managed to turn his head and mouth one word to Sam.

Help.

Chapter Ten

Sunday - Meet the Parents

"MORE mashed potatoes, Gary?" Dad asked, holding out the serving dish.

"Thank you, sir." Gary took them, helped himself to more, and then reached for the gravy. "This is delicious, ma'am."

Sam waited for the sigh.

"It's Moira, dear, and that's Marshall." She met Sam's gaze. "He's a polite one. You could learn a lot from him." That twinkle in her eye spoiled the effect. "And I'm glad you like my cooking, Gary. Sam loves my roast chicken, although lately we've been having it grilled." She peered at his dad. "*Someone* has to watch his weight."

Dad glared at her. "Is nothing sacred? You make it sound like I'm obese." He patted his belly. "There is nothing wrong with a little middle-aged spread."

Sam laughed. "I'd agree, except you left middle age a while back." Before his dad could come back with a reply, he deflected. "How's business been at the store?"

Dad groaned. "If I hear one more customer complain that something is cheaper at the Home Depot, I swear I'll…." He shook his head. "Or else it's, 'Did you know this is on sale at Lowe's?' I was sorely tempted to say to him, 'Then why don't you go back there and buy it?'"

Sam chuckled. "We always get comments like that, right? But the bottom line is people still keep coming back to us. We have loyal customers."

Dad nodded enthusiastically. "It's like I always say. 'Quality will be remembered long—'"

"'—after price is forgotten,'" Sam and Mom chorused, both grinning. Gary was smiling at them all.

Dad gave them a mock scowl. "You two."

Mom snickered and glanced across the dining table at Gary. "So, how did you two meet?"

"Moira. This is Sunday lunch, not an inquisition," his dad remonstrated. "Let the boy eat in peace."

"I was only asking," she retorted. "All I know so far is that they met in Raleigh, and I had to watch a press conference to find *that* out."

"Mom," Sam said, a note of warning in his voice. She gazed back at him innocently, but he wasn't buying that look for a second. He knew her too well. Gary was staring at her calmly enough, but Sam caught the quick bob of his Adam's apple.

"It's obvious," his dad said, waving a forkful of chicken in the air. "They met at a gay bar. I mean, I assume Raleigh has such things." He turned to Sam. "Right?"

Damn. Sam had no idea. When they'd agreed on their story earlier, he hadn't anticipated such an assumption. *Of course he'll think we met in a gay bar.* Maybe Gary wasn't the only one who was nervous.

"Sure, Raleigh has a couple," Gary interjected, his tone light. "There's Flex, Legends, Fifteen. But no, we didn't meet in a gay bar. It was just your ordinary, run-of-the-mill bar." Next to him, Sam put his hand on Gary's leg and gave it a grateful squeeze. Gary acknowledged the gesture with a quick smile. "Actually? We met over a cigarette. I'd snuck out to smoke, and Sam was there, cigarette in hand."

Oh hell.

"Sam smokes?" His mom's gaze bored into him.

Sam removed his hand from Gary's leg and reached for his water glass.

Gary jerked his head to face Sam. "Oh God. Have I just dropped you in it? Babe, I didn't know."

The endearment sounded natural, like it was something Gary always said. Sam knew it was how they'd agreed to play it, but *damn*, it sounded good.

"A little late for that," he muttered.

Gary pierced him with a look. "You didn't cover that part when you wrote the script."

"Maybe cigarettes weren't in the script because I didn't want them mentioned? Hmm?"

His dad burst out laughing. "Lord, anyone can tell you two have been together a while. You argue like an old married couple."

For some reason the thought warmed Sam.

"Anyway, back to my story," Gary continued. "So I was having a cigarette, and Sam joined me. I saw his gaze flicker to my wrist. I wear a rainbow bracelet when I go out for a drink. Raleigh's pretty gay-friendly, though Durham is more open—you can see gay couples walking down the street hand-in-hand there—so it's kind of a code. And it's really useful for scaring off the homophobes too."

"Have you ever encountered anyone like that, Sam?" Mom's voice was quiet. She'd stopped eating and was staring at him in obvious concern.

"Mom, there are always going to be people who think homosexuality is just plain wrong," he said, equally quietly. A pang of guilt stabbed him in the chest, and he resorted to the truth. "But no, I haven't come across many haters." He grimaced. "Though that may change now, of course."

To his surprise, Gary laid his hand over Sam's and laced their fingers together. "I know you're thinking about Hartsell and his crowd, but don't let him spoil your weekend, okay?" His green eyes were warm. "And besides, your lunch is getting cold."

"Good point." Sam peered at their still-joined hands. "Although I may find it easier to eat if you give me my hand back." He smirked and Gary rolled his eyes.

"I can't think why," Gary remarked dryly. "You clearly have no control over it. You can't even hit your mouth accurately." He wet his finger and then reached across to rub it at the corner of Sam's mouth. "But then, it's difficult to get the hang of eating gravy without spilling some, right?" His eyes danced with amusement as he took Sam's napkin and wiped it where he'd applied his finger. "There. All gone."

Sam gave him a look that he hoped promised retribution later. They went back to the business of eating, and thankfully his mom let them.

Sam knew it wasn't the end of the inquisition, merely a reprieve.

"GARY, can I see your ring, please?"

Gary flashed Sam a glance before holding out his left hand.

Mom peered at the ring. "I noticed it during lunch, but all I could tell was it was an older ring." She frowned and gazed at Sam. "Where did you get this? And why is Gary wearing it on the wrong finger?"

Sam's expression was one he hoped Gary could clearly read—*I told you so*—but then he schooled his features. "It was Granddad's ring," he explained. "The one he left to me?"

Mom gave him a superior look. "Have we never heard of resizing?" She let go of Gary's hand and went back to her task of clearing the dishes from the table.

"We agreed not to do that because it was his ring," Sam said. "I felt it was important to leave it as it was."

She nodded. "Yes, I can understand that. It's not like it will matter once you're married, anyway. Then you can *buy* him a ring. One that fits, hopefully."

"Yes, Mom." Sam suppressed his own eye roll, because they tended to get him a smack upside the head.

"And speaking of which…."

Sam's belly churned. He'd known it was coming, of course, and that it couldn't be avoided—that would have been like trying to get out of the path of a tidal wave—but all the same, now that the topic was out there in the open, he was doing his best not to hyperventilate. Mom would see that in a heartbeat.

"Have you set a date yet?"

Gary laughed. "We haven't even given it a thought. Sam has much more important things that take precedence, such as winning an election, for one thing." He arched his eyebrows and grinned. "Right, babe?"

Sam was going to give him such a hug when they got back to Raleigh. "Right. We're not in any hurry." That much was true.

Mom patted Gary on the back. "Gary, thanks for the help cleaning up. I'm going to put your fiancé to work in the kitchen, making the coffee. We'll join you and Marshall in a moment."

"Sure." Gary gave Sam a smile that warmed him inside and went to join his dad in the dining room.

Sam followed his mom into the kitchen, his heart quaking. He knew the signs. She wanted to have A Talk. When she pushed the door until it was almost closed, his heart sank.

God, I hate being right.

"If I close it all the way, your father will only get suspicious and come barging in here, and I don't want us to be interrupted," she said in a low voice. "And as for taking this conversation outside?" She huffed. "Even more suspicious."

"Why all the cloak-and-dagger, Mom?" Sam struggled to keep his cool. Then he winced when she whacked him on the arm, hard. "Hey, what was that for?"

"*That* was for smoking. Filthy habit." She hit him again. "And *that* was for trying to keep it a secret from us."

"Will you stop hitting me, please?" Sam growled out in a low voice. *Lord, and she wonders why I think she's scary.*

"Why didn't you tell us about Gary?" she demanded. "Did you not think we'd want to know that you'd found someone? Even if that someone turned out to be a man? And what about that, hmm? You didn't tell us you were gay." He couldn't miss the hurt in her voice.

"Mom…." He searched for the right words. He'd been mentally preparing for this ever since they'd spoken on the phone, and he thought he'd gotten a handle on it, but now they were finally there, talking about it? Everything he'd prepared flew out of his head. There was only one way to go, and that was with the truth. "Mom, I love you dearly, but you scare the shit out of me. I just wasn't ready to tell you."

"But why? Did you think I wouldn't be able to keep it a secret?"

Sam couldn't help it. He burst out laughing. "Seriously? Mom, I watched you when you worked in the store. You knew *everybody*. And guess what? You *still* know everybody and you still *talk* to everybody. Telling you would be like taking out a full-page ad in the *News & Observer*."

She gasped and clutched her pearls. "I'm not *that* bad."

Sam merely lifted his eyebrows and she huffed.

"Not listening to this. But that wasn't the main reason I dragged you out here." She locked gazes with him. "You and Gary have not been together for a year."

His heartbeat raced and his chest tightened, but he bluffed it out. "I keep forgetting, you *know* everything too. Well, that's all *you* know."

She nodded slowly. "Uh-uh. Call it a mom's intuition. Something just feels slightly... off. I can't put my finger on it, but I know when I'm being sold something. And then there's the whole 'getting engaged at Christmas' part." She arched her thinning eyebrows. "Well?"

Sam sighed and dove headfirst into his lie. "I proposed to him after I'd spent the holidays with you. We just said that because it sounded good for the press—a Christmas engagement, *you* know, romantic...." He held his breath and waited.

Mom pursed her lips. "Okay, I'll buy that. Good publicity and all that. But I'm still not convinced about the length of time you say you've been a couple."

He opened his mouth to speak, to deny it, but she held up her hand.

"Now listen. That being said, you're obviously a good fit."

"Excuse me?" Sam's head spun.

"I've been watching you all afternoon—the way you look at each other, react to each other. Gary's good for you." She snickered. "If I'm being honest here? He's taken years off you. I used to worry that you were growing old before your time, but now? Not so much. Maybe that cougar idea isn't such a bad one. You think your father would object if I traded him in for a younger model?" She grinned mischievously.

"Mom!" *Lord, the things she comes out with sometimes.*

Mom cackled, but then her expression grew more sober. "Seriously, though? I meant what I said. He's a good choice."

"I'm glad you approve." It was all he could manage. "But that still doesn't alter the fact that—"

"Sam? Sweetheart?" She tilted her head. "I can see the two of you being together for many years to come."

What the hell?

"Is that your intuition talking?" His mind was still reeling from her statement.

She nodded again. "So you two need to work on your act, because it's missing something. You might have fooled your dad, but one, he doesn't have my super powers," she said with a grin, "and two, he's on your side. There are going to be others out there who are *not*, and they will be watching you as closely as I was, if not closer." Mom reached up and patted his cheek. "The main thing is? I like him, son. I really do."

"Yeah?" Sam had no idea why that statement filled him with quiet contentment, but it surged through him in a slow wave from his head to his toes.

She nodded once more. "So let's make coffee, and then I'll go spend some more time with my future son-in-law." Her eyes twinkled. "And I was right: he *is* cute."

"Mom!"

GARY was recounting the story of how they'd ditched Steven in Biltmore Village, and both his parents were laughing their asses off. Not that Sam was really listening. He was too busy watching Gary. He really liked the way Gary focused on his parents' faces while he talked, the way he nodded enthusiastically and responded to them. And *damn it*, his mom was right— Gary *was* cute.

They sat next to each other on the couch, their hands entwined on Sam's thigh. It felt like the most natural thing in all the world to be doing, and Sam couldn't help marveling at how his life had changed in less than one week.

Last Sunday evening I was driving to Raleigh, no thought in my head that come Tuesday, I'd be engaged. The situation still had a surreal quality to it.

"Oh my, you didn't." Mom was staring at Gary open-mouthed as he recounted letting the air out of Steven's tires. She giggled. "You know, I could see myself doing something like that."

"I could see it too," both Sam and his dad muttered simultaneously, which had everyone laughing.

It had turned out to be a very pleasant afternoon. Except all good things had to come to an end.

Sam looked at the clock above the fireplace and let out a sigh. "Mom, Dad, we're going to have to leave. We've got to drive back to Raleigh tonight, and that means nearly four hours on the road." Their bags were already in the trunk.

Mom sighed. "If you must. Although while I think about it, next weekend happens to be a very important date. Can't think what it is, exactly, but...."

Sam laughed and turned to Gary to explain, but to his surprise, Gary was way ahead of him. "Oh, right, it's your thirty-fifth wedding anniversary, isn't it?"

Mom beamed. "Yes, dear. And you and Sam are going to join us for the festivities."

"Festivities?" Sam glanced at his dad, who simply sighed. "Mom, what are you planning?"

"A party!" She grinned. "I've invited your aunts and uncles, your cousins, some of our closest friends, my friend Charlotte, who was my maid of honor...." She gave him a hard stare. "And you *are* going to be here. I know it's short notice, but to be honest, I only had the idea this past week."

Sam put two and two together. "Would that be since you found out your only son, the senator, is now engaged?"

"Exactly! So I want you two here so I can show you off. And I want you on your best behavior."

Sam made a supreme effort not to snort, but *damn*, it was a close one. "Fine," he said resignedly, and turned to Gary. "Apparently there's this party we have to attend next weekend."

Gary's eyes sparkled. "Can't wait."

Sam had the feeling the week was going to speed by.

"Son? Can I ask you something?"

Sam gazed at his dad. "Sure."

Dad shifted in his armchair, crossing and uncrossing his ankles. His face was tight. "I haven't said anything so far today because I was waiting for you to say something first. But seeing as that hasn't happened, I can't let you leave without getting something off my chest." He glanced at Mom. "I'm sure your mom has already had words. If she hasn't, then someone had better inform the media, because the world might just be about to end." He ignored Mom's gasp and fixed his gaze on Sam. "Why didn't you tell your mom and me that you were gay? And don't you think we deserved to learn that about our son in a conversation, rather than hearing it on TV in a *press conference*?"

There was suddenly a lump in this throat. "Sir, I…."

"Sam was afraid of disappointing you both, Marshall," Gary blurted out, his hand tightening around Sam's. He gave Sam a warm look, full of compassion. "He didn't want you to look at him with different eyes," he said softly. "I can understand that.

He loves you both so much that he couldn't bear the thought of your disapproval."

Sam's heart quaked. *Fuck. He sees me.*

Then his dad cleared his throat and the moment was lost.

Dad's expression softened. "Sam, we don't love you any less because you're gay. But it isn't something you should have hidden." His eyes glistened. "Never be ashamed for who you are. And if there are people out there who can't love you for that? Well, they don't deserve to be in your life."

Mom was quiet, but she nodded, her eyes moist.

It took Sam a moment or two to find his voice. "Thank you. I'm sorry it took me so long."

"Better late than never," Mom said with a smile.

Sam glanced across at Gary, their hands still entwined. "There's another reason why I kept quiet, you know."

"Oh?" Gary's gaze was focused on Sam's face.

Sam nodded. "I was afraid of what my constituents would say if they knew. But to be fair, no one ever caught my eye before, so it wasn't worth taking the chance."

"Have I caught your eye, Senator?" The words were uttered softly, as if only for Sam's ears. Sam knew it was an act for his parents' benefit, but *damn*, the light in Gary's eyes, that expression on his face, as if no one else existed for him in that bubble of time but Sam….

Mom broke the spell. "Now, you two need to go."

Sam looked toward her, and she smiled as though she knew exactly what he'd been thinking in that precious moment.

"It's not like we have to wait too long until we see you again, is it?" she said practically. "Next weekend will be here before you know it. The party is on Saturday night, and you can stay over. I'll put you both in Sam's old room."

She rose, and Dad did too. It was time for good-byes.

It wasn't until they were in the car and pulling out of the driveway that Sam got the feeling he'd missed something. His mind went back over the last few minutes of conversation. Something about next Saturday….

Gary and I will be sharing a room? No. That wasn't it. Then it hit him.

We'll be sharing a bed.
Oh Lord.

Chapter Eleven

Monday, Monday....

SAM switched off the engine and huffed out a breath.

Beside him, Gary chuckled. "The day hasn't even started yet and already you seem out of sorts. What's up?"

Sam didn't want to share what was uppermost in his mind—that their weekend was over, the dream was shattered, and that reality was banging on his door, demanding to be let in. Spending time with Gary had been wonderful, and Sam was surprised to realize he didn't want it to come to an end.

"I suppose it's that Monday morning feeling we all get," he said at last. "Senators aren't immune, after all."

"I know what you mean." Gary expelled a sigh. "I have a couple hours here on the phones, and then it's off to classes."

"I thought you weren't going to work the phones anymore?"

Gary snorted. "No, *Josh* said I wasn't going to work the phones anymore. Look, I know we've got a couple of talk shows lined up for the end of the week, but I am not going to sit around on my a—chair, waiting to be photographed, interviewed, poked, etc. I need to keep busy." He smiled. "And besides, working the phones makes me feel like I'm doing something practical to help you win this election. It's just a good thing the people at the other end won't know it's your fiancé they're talking to. I'd never get off the damn thing." He reached out and stroked Sam's thigh. "It's not going to be easy, though. I've sort of gotten used to you being around." His expression grew gloomy. "But this is real life, I guess. We've got to get used to it."

No, we damn well don't.

"Says who?" Sam demanded. When Gary arched his eyebrows, Sam continued. "You think I'm going to go home this evening and sit in my log cabin, wondering what you're up to? Uh-uh."

"What did you have in mind, Senator?" Gary's eyes gleamed.

"Josh suggested you stay with me as much as possible, so let's make the man happy. How about you meet me here when your classes are done and you come home with me? I'll cook us dinner, and you can spend the night. If you want to, of course."

"If I want to," Gary echoed with a chuckle. "For a supposedly intelligent man, you sure say some dumb things sometimes. Of course I want to. I'm picking up my car from the shop after my shift, so I'll drive back and leave it here tonight." He leaned forward and kissed the tip of Sam's nose. "Great idea."

The gesture sent a ripple of warmth through Sam. "And you can join me for coffee before you leave here. Come on up to the office and I'll take a break."

"You're on." Gary grinned. "Of course, what I'm dying to know is if things have changed in there." He nodded toward the house.

"What do you mean?"

"The last time I worked a shift on the phones, I was plain old Gary Mason. *Now* I'm the senator's fiancé. It will be interesting to see their reactions." Sam frowned, and Gary quickly laid a hand on his thigh. "Hey, I don't anticipate any problems—these guys love you, remember?—but I'm expecting some playful banter and any amount of teasing."

Sam snorted. "Sucks to be you." They got out of the car, Sam locked it, and they walked into the house. The sound of lively chatter was already audible from the phones room. Sam patted Gary on the arm and headed for the stairs, but Gary stopped him.

"You're out and proud now, Senator Dalton," he said with a smile. "And that means you get to leave your fiancé with a kiss." He tapped his cheek with his index finger. "Right here will do."

Sam laughed. "You're enjoying this, aren't you?" He moved closer and kissed Gary on the cheek, his skin scratchy with stubble. Sam grinned. "You need a shave, mister."

Gary waggled his eyebrows. "In answer to your question? Oh yeah, I'm loving every minute of this." He leaned up and returned the kiss. "See you at coffee time." And with that he disappeared into the phones room.

Sam shook his head, unable to wipe the smile from his face. He was still smiling when he walked through the door into his office. "Good morning, Becky. Coffee, please."

Becky poked her head around her door. "My, my, look at you, Mr. Cat Who Got the Cream. *Someone's* had a good few days away from the office." Her grin was positively evil. "I'll be out in a second with your coffee."

Sam took off his coat, hung it up, and sat behind his desk. That last encounter with Gary had left him with a warm glow, one he was determined to hold on to for as long as possible.

Curtis entered the office, his forehead furrowed. "We need to talk."

Sam raised his eyebrows. "And good morning to you too."

Curtis flopped down into the chair facing Sam's desk and leaned back. "Good morning. And now that we've gotten the social niceties out of the way, where's your partner in crime?"

"Excuse me?"

Curtis stared. "You know, the guy who lets air out of people's tires? I swear, I have never heard Josh so pissed. Whose idea was that, by the way?"

"His." Sam grinned. "Mine was ditching Steven and making a run for it."

Curtis nodded. "Amazing. You got engaged to Gary on Tuesday and by Friday he'd managed to regress you into a schoolboy." When Sam stared at him in amazement, Curtis snorted. "Oh, come on. You weren't that childish even in high school. I'm beginning to think he's a bad influence on you."

"You'd have an argument from my mom on that one."

Curtis's eyes widened. "Oh my God. The world is about to end. Moira likes him."

"Oh yes. She thinks he's taken years off me."

At that moment Becky came in with two mugs of coffee. She deposited them on the desk and quickly retreated into her office, closing the door behind her.

Sam frowned. "What's up with her?" Usually Becky would stay and chat with them.

"Your loyal secretary obviously follows social media, unlike you."

Sam had been clinging to his good mood by his fingertips, but the edge crumbled away with that last comment. "Okay, you have my attention. What's going on?"

Curtis scrolled through on his phone. "It's not all bad news."

"Oh, great," Sam groaned. "There's bad news?"

Curtis merely peered at him intently. "I'll go on, shall I? The photos on various social media platforms were paying off. Saturday evening we did a quick online poll, and your popularity among the younger voters was significantly improved. The Twitter and Instagram initiatives in particular had gained a very favorable reaction."

"I'm sensing a 'but' on the horizon."

Curtis nodded. "That made its appearance last night. Hartsell put out a statement, and all our good work was virtually wiped out."

Sam's heart sank. "That must have been one hell of a statement. Why am I only hearing about this now?"

"Because we didn't want to disturb you, that's why!" Curtis got up from his chair and paced a little. "Those selfies you guys took in the Blue Ridge Parkway?" He let out a sigh. "I haven't seen you look that relaxed in a long time. Can you blame me for not wanting to burst your bubble?" He handed Sam the phone. "Especially when they were exactly what Hartsell was using against you."

Sam stared at the screen. Just the length of the post had his chest tightening.

This is not going to be good.

The post was headed with a banner showing the pastor sitting at a desk, looking pensive.

I'm taking a moment from a busy schedule to share with you some of the activities and events that I've been proud to participate in this last week. As many of you will know, I take an active interest in what goes on in my native state. I've been blessed to meet with so many constituents, to hear their views and take on board their suggestions for where they feel attention should be paid.

So what have I been doing this last week?

I attended a forum on climate change and a rally on the importance of family values in modern-day America. I visited a couple of our high schools to talk with students about their futures. I met with business leaders and representatives from the various industries that flourish here in North Carolina, such as aviation, green and sustainable energy, and pharmaceuticals.

Now that I write it all down, I see just how busy I was.

And in the meantime, what did Senator Samuel Dalton do with his week? Let's take a look, shall we?

He bathed a dog. Cleaned out kitty boxes. Walked a dog.

He went for a hike in the Blue Ridge Parkway.

He did some shopping in the Biltmore Village.

He visited the Biltmore Estate, apparently with a view to using it as a possible wedding venue.

Oh, and he and his fiancé were the subject of countless photos. It seemed every time I opened a magazine or scrolled through social media, there he was.

Now, I understand the necessity of promotion. It's a beast all public figures must harness and employ as best we can. But this was excessive, to say the least, and I know from talking to the countless people I met during my week that I'm not the only one who thinks this way. We grew heartily tired of seeing these contrived images everywhere we looked.

But surely, with an election coming up, there were things that should have taken precedence over dog-bathing and window-shopping? I don't know about you good people out there, but I for one am thinking that these activities, while clearly pleasurable, did little to serve the constituents of North Carolina.

Sam slowly raised his head to stare at Curtis. "Damn, he's a clever son of a bitch, isn't he?" He handed over the phone. "Whatever I do, he's the one who comes up smelling of roses. It doesn't matter what engagements I have this week—they'll simply be seen as me reacting to this post. Everything he said I did is true—there are the photos to back it up. He doesn't make it a personal attack; he sticks to the facts. Although I do wonder what number constitutes 'countless' people. He was a little too vague on that point."

"Yeah, I noticed." Curtis huffed. "And you're right. There's no way to come back on any of this."

"It may also be an indication that we've reached saturation point with the photos. I sure didn't miss that 'contrived' barb, and I'm guessing you didn't either. Better make sure Josh is aware of this."

"Oh, he's aware, all right. Steven was due to take more photos this week, but I think Josh has canceled it."

Curtis scrolled through once more. "I'd only scheduled a couple of events, but in the light of this, do you want me to schedule more?"

Sam shook his head. "That'll make matters worse. We don't want to play into his hands any more than we already have done."

The outer door was flung open, and Gary burst in, his face flushed. "Have you seen what that ba—"

"Yes, yes," Sam assured him quickly. "Now shut the door and take a seat."

Gary did as instructed. "I take it Josh has already come up with a rebuttal?"

There was an uneasy silence.

Gary looked from Sam to Curtis and back to Sam again. "Guys? You can't mean you're just going to do nothing?" His face darkened. "You can't let him get away with this!"

"Gary, there isn't a lot we can—"

Gary glared at Curtis. "Sure there is. There has to be."

Curtis set his jaw. "Look, I know you feel involved, but you're—"

"You're *damn right* I feel involved." Gary's eyes flashed and he turned to Sam. "Hartsell's always going on about family, right? Well, once we're married, *we* will be family. It'll be a damn sight more family than I've got right now, that's for sure. And that's what last week was: spending time with your *family*, Senator." He lunged to his feet. "So you'd better come up with something to throw back at him, because silence just plays right into his hands. And while you're at it? You might want to do some investigating, because I already have. This 'forum' he attended on climate change? It was organized by the Kellem Foundation."

Sam stared at him, Curtis did too, and Gary nodded. "Yeah, that was my reaction. Seems like the good pastor is being a little economical with the truth, wouldn't you say? That might be something you feel should be shared with these 'countless people' he was talking about." He patted his pockets. "Why is it when I really need a cigarette, I don't have them on me?"

"I thought we were quitting," Sam said with a half smile. Seeing Gary so passionate, so... vital, had stirred something inside him.

He's ready to fight for me.

The least Sam could do would be to do the same.

"So I'll quit tomorrow," Gary said, his eyes glinting. "I need one."

Sam nodded and stood. "So do I." He glanced at Curtis. "We're going to go outside for one cigarette, and when we come back, the three of us—four, if we can get Josh in here—are going to put our heads together and come up with something. Because Gary's right. Doing nothing isn't an option."

Gary stared at him, a slow smile creeping over his face.

Curtis met his gaze, and for a moment, neither of them spoke. Then he nodded. "Fine. Go fill up your lungs with foul-smelling smoke. When you've both sucked on a breath mint, *then* we'll talk."

Sam chuckled. "See, *now* I see why you don't make the speeches. We won't be long." He guided Gary out of the office, down the stairs, through the kitchen, and out into the cool early February morning.

Gary leaned on the porch wall and sucked in a few deep breaths of fresh air. "I'm sorry for barging in like that, but when someone showed me what he'd been saying, I saw red."

"So if I were to say that seeing you support me like that was incredibly sweet, touching, stirring….?"

Gary moved closer, until Sam could feel the warmth of his body through his shirt. "You listened to me," he said quietly.

"Of course I listened to you. Why wouldn't I?" Anything else he'd been about to say was lost when Gary placed a finger against Sam's lips.

"Sam? Stop talking? I want to kiss you."

Then Sam stopped breathing when Gary's lips met his, soft as a whisper, warm and inviting. Gary cupped Sam's head, his body pressed up against Sam's, firm and sexy as hell.

When they parted, Sam felt drunk. "I know I have nothing to compare you with, but…." He could hear the tremor in his own voice. "I love the way you kiss."

Gary smiled. "I love the way you kiss back." He pulled away. "Now, wasn't that better than a cigarette?"

Sam was having a hard time keeping up. *That kiss must have addled my brains.* Then it dawned on him. "You didn't come down here for a smoke, did you?"

Gary's smile was wicked. "I figured you'd come with me."

"Are you saying I'm predictable?" Sam speared him with a glance. "Just remember—I know where you're sleeping tonight."

Oh hell.

Gary's lips parted. His eyes shone. His tongue darted out to lick his lips. His skin flushed above the collar of his shirt. Slowly he nodded. "In the room next to yours," he said quietly.

Sam coughed. "Maybe we should get back to work." *Anything* rather than confront the way Gary had just made him feel.

Not ready for this.

"WELL?" Sam demanded. Beside him, Gary was focused on Curtis too.

Curtis looked up from Sam's monitor and smiled. "I like it. How about we try it out on a volunteer?" Before Sam could react, Curtis raised his voice. "Becky? Get in here."

"What now?" She bustled into the office. "You've been through two pots of coffee already."

Sam pointed to an empty chair. "Sit."

Becky complied, her eyebrows lifted so high they almost disappeared into her hairline. "I am *not* Dinky," she said huffily.

"No, you're not," Sam agreed. He caught Gary's eye and winked. "At least Dinky could be trained."

He could have sworn he heard Becky growl.

Josh cleared his throat. "We want to read something to you before we publish it. Get your reaction, okay?"

She nodded. "Go for it."

Josh gave a cough and began to read. Sam felt Gary's hand curl around his.

Pastor Hartsell has been campaigning about family values and how they're the bedrock of civilization. He has a good point, and it's one of the things on which we are in agreement. During the past five days, however, I tried to spend time with my family, but according to the pastor, this was wrong. In the six years that I have represented the citizens of this state, I have always given my all, but at the same time, I will always make time for my family—including the man I'm going to marry. Because if we don't find the time to do that, what are we really working for?

My parents are the reason that I'm able to represent you in the General Assembly. My father works at the store my great-grandfather opened, while I'm fighting for your *families.*

I'm sorry to have to break this to you good people, but I'm only human. I can provide you with my calendar for the last six years. You'll see where I've been, what I've been doing—and how long it's been since I've taken some time away from being your representative. And that's what I was doing these past few days: taking time away from my work to spend it with my family. I'm sharing this in the hope that you'll understand my desire to have it all: a job I love, and a family I love just as much. Like I said, I'm only human.

We all agree that climate change is one of the biggest threats to the stability of our planet. For years now, countries have been striving to bring down their CO_2 emissions in a bid to halt this change. Pastor Hartsell says that he was attending a forum on climate change, and that's true: he was. He was the keynote speaker for the Kellem Foundation, the very same people who deny climate change is real. I'd be the first to admit I don't have all the answers on this one, but I have to trust our scientists when they say we're impacting the future of your children and, maybe one day, ours.

Take a moment today to reach out to those you love, those you consider family. They are what matters, after all.

Josh fell silent. The four men turned to gauge Becky's reaction.

To Sam's surprise she wiped her eyes with the sleeve of her blouse. "Don't you change one word of that," she said roughly. "And if you'll excuse me? I want to call my kids." She disappeared back into her office.

Sam met Josh's gaze. "Run it," he said simply.

Josh grinned. "With pleasure, boss."

Chapter Twelve

Monday night

"I LOVED what you said in that post, you know," Gary said quietly, his gaze focused on the flickering flames. He was curled up on the couch, a glass of red wine in his hand and Sam beside him.

Perfect.

Sam inclined his head to regard him. "You helped write it, remember? And it was your comments about family that gave me the idea." He sipped his wine. "I guess we'll have to wait and see if it had an impact. We might get an indication of that tomorrow."

Gary wracked his brains, but nothing was forthcoming. "Okay, pretend like I've forgotten. What's tomorrow?"

"I'm at Duke University tomorrow afternoon for a Q&A session, and there's a mixer afterward. You could come with me. I'm sure that would go down well with the students attending the session." He smiled. "What am I saying? You *are* coming with me. Josh's instructions."

For one brief moment, the words were right on the tip of Gary's tongue. *How about me being there because you want me there?* "I have classes in the morning," he said when he found his voice.

Sam stretched out a hand and squeezed his knee. "Forget what Josh said; *I'd* really like it if you could come along." He uttered the words softly, the firelight catching in his dark eyes.

Like Gary could resist that.

"Sure, I'll come."

Sam's face glowed, and Gary wasn't entirely sure it was because of the fire. "Thank you. We can meet at the office and you can travel there with me and Josh." He took another drink of wine. "This is really nice."

"It is," Gary agreed. Dinner had been simple but delicious, and sitting on the couch, letting the evening slowly tick by, was heavenly. He knew he'd need to sleep soon, but having Sam all to himself was too good an opportunity to pass up, especially when there was something on his mind.

No time like the present.

"I have a confession," he began, shifting his position until he was sitting at a right angle to Sam, his bare feet propped up on Sam's thigh.

"Should I be worried?" Sam said with the hint of a smile.

"It's about Sunday." Gary took a sip of wine and plunged forward. "I… I heard what your mom said to you in the kitchen."

Sam stared. "Oh?" He leaned forward and put his glass on the floor next to the couch. "All of it or a particular part?"

"The bit about not believing we'd been together a year. I agree with her. We need to work on our act." *Only that's not how it feels, is it?*

"Our act?" The questioning tone in Sam's voice caught Gary off guard. "Ah, I see."

Gary took hold of his courage with both hands. "No, I don't think you do." He put his own glass down and moved closer to Sam. "Just for the record?" He looked Sam in the eye. "I like you. I like you a lot." *In fact, I could really like you a whole lot more.*

"I like you too."

"But your mom's not that far off base. We knew saying we'd been together a year would be pushing it. Sure, we've had to sidestep a couple of questions, but we did it. Your mom is right, though. We work well together. But I think we could improve even on that."

Sam was silent, his gaze fixed on Gary, his breathing just that little bit quicker.

I'm going to have to make the first move here, aren't I?

"Care to try a little experiment?" Gary asked.

"Okay." The cautious tone wasn't lost on Gary, but Sam's staccato breaths set his own heart racing.

He knelt up and leaned closer, his hand on the back of the couch to support himself. Slowly he brought their mouths together in a kiss—soft, tender, chaste. Sam kissed him back. Emboldened, Gary parted Sam's lips with his tongue and kissed him again. He registered the change in Sam's breathing instantly. Gary pulled back. "Tell me what you're thinking," he whispered. Before Sam could reply, he moved in for another kiss, sliding his tongue into Sam's mouth, conscious of the tiniest moan that escaped Sam. Gary drew back once more. "Tell me how you feel."

Sam gazed at him, pupils so large and black. "Relaxed," he admitted.

It was a start.

Gary kissed him again, this time making it a lot more sensual, and his heart soared when Sam slipped his arms around him and held him, kissing him back. They sat like that until Gary had lost all track of time, lost in kiss after slow kiss, both of them taking their time. He was like a rock in his jeans, but he ignored it. When Sam shifted and Gary felt hardness against his hip, he knew he had to do something.

With reluctance he pulled away. "Let's leave it there for tonight." His voice was husky.

"Why?" Sam was hoarse too.

Gary stroked his cheek. "We might be engaged, but this is still new to you, right? I don't want to push you too hard, too fast."

Sam stared at him, lips parted. "And what if I *want* you to push me too hard, too fast?"

Gary placed his hand on Sam's chest, feeling the rapid heartbeat. He grinned. "Which head is doing the talking right now?"

Sam's low noise of disappointment was gratifying.

"The little one," he muttered, cheeks flushed.

"And that's good," Gary said. "But until it's the big head talking, we need to slow down."

"Could we *go* any slower?" Sam groaned.

Gary stroked Sam's cheek once more. "This is not the end, all right? We can do this again."

Sam nodded. He lifted his head to look Gary in the face. "So what have you learned from your experiment?" The rapid rise and fall of his chest told Gary much.

"That you and I have chemistry, Senator." *And that maybe one day soon this will stop being an act and become a whole lot more real.*

Gary couldn't wait.

SAM closed his bedroom door and within seconds his jeans were open, his hand was wrapped around his hard cock, and he was pumping it for all he was worth. He shuffled across to the bed, dropped down onto it on his back, and shoved his jeans lower. Sam closed his eyes and let his hand do the talking.

Fuck, those kisses.

Sam had never been so turned on in his life. He cupped his balls and squeezed them gently, his hand not slowing for a second. He was so close. It had taken all his effort and concentration to hold on until he'd reached the sanctuary of his room. Holding Gary, kissing him, God, the *feel* of him in Sam's arms.

Sam tugged harder, his balls churning, that electricity sparking up and down his spine until he was coming, back arched up off the bed, mouth open wide in a silent cry. He lay there shivering as the last remnants of his orgasm jolted their way through his body.

For the first time in his life, Sam was close to actually having sex, and *damn it*, the thought had his gut in knots. Not that it was a bombshell—reaching the age of thirty-three with his virginity intact pointed to a whole lot of reticence and more than his fair share of fear. But that fear of intimacy was tempered by the knowledge that his first time would be with Gary. He knew it was inevitable now; even if the marriage idea didn't work out, Sam was finally going to get laid. What really surprised the hell out of him was the feeling growing inside him that Gary would make it good. Gary would take care of him.

He pulled off his shirt and used it to wipe away his come before dropping it into the laundry hamper. He walked into his bathroom and, standing before the mirror, that white light illuminating his face so starkly, Sam stared at his reflection.

He likes me. Gary's words had sent a pang that cut right through his heart. Sam might have repeated them back, but he already knew them to be a lie.

Sam had passed merely liking Gary a while back. This was something else entirely.

SAM looked out into the audience that filled the Baldwin Auditorium to capacity—even the balcony was packed. There had to be at least six hundred students and staff in front of him. Gary was sitting on the front row, grinning at him throughout the entire session, occasionally giving him the thumbs-up.

"Okay, are there any more questions?" Sam asked into the microphone. He'd been impressed thus far. The students had shown a keen interest in his life as a senator, and the topics had ranged from the environment to economics to his plans for the future.

A young man toward the back raised his hand, and one of the stewards passed him the wireless mic. "So how does it feel to be out, Senator?" He grinned.

Sam was amazed it had taken that long. "It feels great," he said with a smile. "Gary and I—give them a wave, Gary."

Gary looked around and waved, which brought a brief burst of applause from the audience.

"We're glad everything is finally out in the open. Pun intended."

There were chuckles from some of the audience. Another student raised her hand. "Any idea when the wedding will be?"

"As yet, we haven't fixed a date."

"Any plans to adopt Dinky, Senator?"

Laughter rippled through the crowd.

Sam narrowed his eyes at Gary. "Did you put him up to that?"

More laughter followed.

Gary widened his eyes. "I swear! I'm totally innocent."

Those around him were laughing.

"Yeah, right." Sam raised his head to address the audience. "He's looking at me with those puppy-dog eyes, except I know better. I saw that same expression last evening. I went to the cookie jar to get the last one of my favorite peanut butter cookies, and what do you know? It was gone." He peered intently at Gary, who was clearly biting back laughter. "When I confronted him about it, do you know what he said to me?" Sam affected an innocent expression. "'We have mice, Sam.'"

An explosion of chuckling and cackling followed.

Sam grinned at his audience. "Yeah, you're not buying it either, are you?" From the side, Josh caught his eye and indicated the clock. Sam nodded. "Okay, we have time for one more question."

A young woman about three rows from the front raised her hand and was passed the mic. She cleared her throat, her face flushing. "I actually had my question all worked out when this session was first announced last month. I was gonna ask for your phone number." Hoots of laughter followed, and she turned around, her cheeks bright pink. "Yeah, then I saw the press conference last week and I thought 'Aw, shi—shoot.'" More laughter erupted, and Sam joined in. The young woman's face was a picture. "So, here's my new question: Do you and Gary plan on having children?"

Sam was taken aback. There was a fluttery feeling in his belly, and he looked out to see Gary's response. The calm smile on Gary's face made his heart soar.

"I'd love to have kids one day," Sam said quietly. Gary nodded immediately, and Sam's skin tingled all over. "I know there are lots of kids out there just waiting to be adopted, and I think it would be great to give one a home. As for how many? Not a clue."

To his surprise, Gary raised his hand. When he had the mic, Gary looked Sam in the eye. "Speaking personally, I'd like at least two. I grew up an only child, and when I was thirteen, I lost my parents."

Sam stared at him in amazement. He nodded enthusiastically for Gary to continue.

When Gary spoke again, his voice was stronger, more confident. "I think life would have been easier if I'd had siblings, someone to share with, to love, when things got too dark. And I second Sam's idea of adoption. I think it's a wonderful notion, but I have to be honest here. I'd prefer to go down the surrogacy route, because if we have kids? I'd want them to look like Sam."

Sam's throat was suddenly tight as he listened to the chorus of *aws* from around the auditorium.

"Hey, Senator?" It was the guy from earlier. He gave Sam the thumbs-up. "The kids would love to have a dog. Just saying."

In the front row, Gary burst out laughing and was soon joined by others.

The session organizer, Dr. Hockland, stepped up to the mic. "I'm sorry, but that really is all we have time for. Would you please join me in thanking Senator Dalton for stopping by today and answering our questions with such frankness, honesty, and humor?"

Applause broke out instantly, and soon the auditorium rang with its sound. Sam raised his hand to accept it, smiling and nodding, grateful for the reprieve. There was no way he could have gotten a word out just then.

When the applause died down, Dr. Hockland spoke into the mic once more. "Those of you with tickets to the mixer, you have thirty minutes before you're expected at the Student Life Conference Room. Thank you, everyone, for making this an enjoyable event."

Her words were followed by noise and chatter as students began to leave the auditorium. She turned to Sam, hand extended. "That was wonderful, Senator. I'll give you a moment to get your breath back before I whisk you across campus to the venue for the mixer. I take it Mr. Mason will be accompanying you?" Her eyes twinkled. "For moral support."

Gary was waiting by the stairs off to the right of the stage, still smiling.

"Yes, he'll be with me."

Sam wanted Gary at his side, and not just for moral support either.

He was starting to believe that was where Gary belonged.

"HAVE I told you how wonderful you were yet?" Gary murmured, his hand resting on Sam's back, just above his waist, while he sipped from a glass of wine.

Sam snickered. "About three times so far, but please, tell me again. I love praise."

Gary snorted. "If we weren't in polite company right now, I'd swat you on the ass," he muttered under his breath.

"You could try," Sam said darkly.

He was glad of the lull in the proceedings. They'd mingled with staff and students, and the atmosphere had been relaxed, but they'd answered informal questions for about an hour. There had been several photo opportunities too, and Sam's facial muscles were starting to ache.

He was ready to go home.

"Senator Dalton?"

Sam turned to see a young woman with an earnest expression next to him. He peered at her name badge. "Hello, Kimberley," he greeted her politely. Then he caught sight of another badge on the shoulder strap of her purse—Christians on Campus.

"I have a question for you, if that's okay." Her voice was loud and clear, and several heads turned in their direction.

"Of course." Sam felt Gary's hand slip into his, and he squeezed it, silently thanking him for the support.

"It's about your upcoming marriage, Senator. Why should North Carolina be represented by someone who

ignores the basic tenet of the Bible, that marriage is
between a man and a woman?"

Hell.

Before he could open his mouth, she pressed on.
"Christians make up nearly 50 percent of this state,
Senator. Why should they support someone who clearly
does not represent them?"

Sam took a deep breath. "I'm sure not every one
of the 47.51 percent of Christians in North Carolina—
yes, I *am* aware of the exact figure—believes as you
do, Kimberley, but we'll leave that aside for the
moment. They should support me because I represent
them, just as I represent 51.3 percent of constituents
who are women. Am I a woman? No. I also represent
the 22 percent of people in the state who are Black or
African American. The 14 percent who are over the
age of sixty-five. The nearly thirty thousand same-sex
couples who reside in North Carolina. The miners in
the Appalachians. The farmers. The coastal fishermen."
He locked gazes with her. "It's my job to represent
everyone, and surely that demands their support."
There were murmurs of support and approval from
those nearest, and Kimberley's face flushed.

Sam leaned closer. "It might surprise you to learn
that I was brought up to love God. And I believe He
loves *all* His children, regardless of their ethnicity or
their sexual orientation."

"Sounds like my God too," said a quiet voice from
next to Gary.

Kimberley swallowed. "Thank you, Senator." She
walked away stiffly.

Sam turned to the speaker, a young man in a pale
blue sweater.

"I wanted to thank you for coming here day," he said to Sam. "It meant a lot to me."

"Oh?" Beside him, Gary moved closer.

The young man—Michael—nodded shyly. "We need more people in government who aren't afraid to… be themselves." Another student joined them, and it only took Sam one glance to realize they were a couple.

He peered at the badge below Michael's name tag. "What does CSGD stand for?"

"The Center for Sexual and Gender Diversity," Michael said. "It provides a lot of things, but mainly a space for LGBTQI students and staff." He inclined his head toward his partner. "It's where I met Riley." He gazed at Sam with shining eyes. "And what you wrote yesterday about family? That last line said it all. You talked about 'those you consider family.' Sometimes we're closer to people who aren't our flesh and blood. Sometimes it's your flesh-and-blood family who let you down when you need them most."

His words made Sam's heart ache. He'd been so fortunate with his parents.

The representative of the *Chronicle*, the University's daily student newspaper, approached them with her camera. "Can I take a picture of you two with the senator and Mr. Mason?"

Sam looked at Michael, who shook his head.

Riley paled. "Lord, no. Suppose my parents got to see it? They wouldn't even like the idea of me coming to this meeting."

"You're not out at home?" Gary asked quietly, and Riley shook his head.

Sam smiled at the photographer. "No, thanks." She walked away, and he turned to Riley and Michael. "Thank you for coming to talk with us here."

There was that shy smile again. "No, thank you. We want to wish you all the luck with your future wedding and your life together." He held out his hand, and Sam shook it.

He watched the two young men walk away, and something deep inside him ached.

"What is it? What's wrong?" Gary leaned closer.

Sam let out a sigh. "I was actually thinking I wish I'd been brave enough to come out at his age, instead of being afraid of going into politics as a gay man. I missed out on so much."

Gary's hand found his. "Two things. You got there eventually, and surely that's a good thing. And if you'd come out sooner, your life might have turned out very different." He looked into Sam's eyes. "I might never have met you, for one thing."

Damn. It was possibly the sweetest thing Gary could have said.

Chapter Thirteen

Thursday

"WHERE'S Gary today?" Curtis asked as he entered Sam's office. "He's not on the phones."

"No, he has classes all day." Sam had hardly seen him the previous day, and he hadn't stayed the night since Monday. Sam had been listless all Wednesday evening, unable to fathom why, until finally it had struck him: he missed Gary.

Sam was suddenly aware of how quiet his office had become.

He glanced up to find Curtis staring at him. "What?"

Curtis walked over to Becky's door and peered around it. "Okay, where's Grace?" he joked.

"She's gone for the afternoon. Doctor's appointment. Why?" Then he thought about it. "I always saw her more as Karen, myself."

Curtis grabbed the Meeting in Progress door hanger and hung it outside. Then he closed the door and sat in the chair facing Sam's desk. "Okay, talk to me."

"About what?" Sam had an awful feeling he knew where this was leading. He'd never been able to hide anything from Curtis, even when they were in high school.

Curtis arched his eyebrows. "How long have we been friends?"

Sam ignored him. "Why were you looking for Gary?"

"I wanted to show him some of the drafts for the magazine articles featuring you two. Josh just gave them to me. They look really good. Oh, and to ask for his bank details so we can arrange payment."

Payment. "Are we paying off all his loans and tuition fees at the same time?"

Curtis shook his head. "I talked with him last week. We'll pay off the loans now. We'll wait until September when he starts at vet school to pay his tuition." He grinned. "Of course, you could be married by then." The grin faded and he tilted his head. "And don't think I haven't noticed you trying to avoid my question. I've known you long enough to know when something isn't right."

Sam didn't know where—or how—to begin.

"How are you and Gary getting along?" Curtis asked him. "Josh was really impressed by your Q&A at Duke the other day, by the way. He said it was difficult to believe you weren't a real couple."

And there it was.

"Sam?" Curtis's voice was quiet. "What is it?"

Sam's heart pounded. "What if… what if I want to make it real?" Without allowing Curtis to reply, Sam shook his head. "This is madness. I've known him for nearly eleven days. That's all, eleven days."

"So? What does that matter?" Curtis leaned back, his gaze fixed on Sam. "You really like him, don't you?"

Sam nodded. "He's funny, Curtis. He makes me laugh so much. And he's smart too."

"He'd have to be if they're going to let him train to be a vet. Got to have brains for that."

"And he's really good with people. You should have seen him at that reception. And oh my God, Mom and Dad—he handled that so well."

Curtis stared at him. "So what's stopping you?"

Sam jerked his head up. "Huh?"

"What's stopping you from making it real?" He chuckled. "The ball's in your court, Sam. You're engaged to him. You've announced that you're planning to marry, even if you haven't set a date yet. You can make this as real as you want it. Providing, of course, he wants that too."

"Yeah, but that's the issue here. He didn't sign up for a real relationship, did he? He signed up to get his debts paid off. To be seen with me. To be Senator Dalton's husband in name only."

"Wait a moment." Curtis got up from his chair and paced, like he always did when he was trying to figure something out. "Let's go back to what Josh said, about you two seeming like a real couple. Rapport like that takes two, Sam. There has to be some connection there, some chemistry."

Sam knew that all he had to do was close his eyes, and he'd be back on that couch, with Gary in his arms, making out. He couldn't repress the shiver that trickled down his spine.

"I don't think I want to know what you just thought about," Curtis said with a snicker. "Because I have a sneaking suspicion it was dirty. And best friends or not, I draw the line at hearing tales of your sex life, okay?"

Sam smiled. "You have no worries on that score, believe me."

Curtis laughed. "I think you're worrying about nothing, Sam. Circumstances pushed the two of you together, and happily for you, things are working out better than you'd ever hoped. Think about it. What's better, to find yourself married to a guy who you don't get along with—where there's no chemistry, no shared interests, no nothing—or to find yourself with a partner who complements you, who you clearly like, and if that little shiver was anything to go by, who does it for you in other areas too?" He stared at Sam intently. "And la, la, la, I *still* don't want to know."

Sam grinned. "But I get to hear about all *your* conquests," he teased. "How stacked they are, how eager…. It only seems fair that I reciprocate." Not that he had the slightest intention of doing so.

"Only if you want to lose your best friend," Curtis muttered. "Sam, I love you like a brother, but I do *not* want to have pictures of you and Gary in my head, okay? You gay, me straight, and never the twain shall meet. Got it?"

"Got it."

Curtis got up from his chair. "I think I preferred it when you were in the closet," he said under his breath. "It was a whole lot less traumatic."

Sam snorted. "You and Josh opened this Pandora's box, remember? Deal with it." He peered at him.

"Haven't you got some staff to go shout at? That's what you do here, isn't it?" He was enjoying himself.

Curtis gave him a superior look. "Fine." He got as far as the door before turning back to gaze at Sam. "You *do* know how happy I am for you, don't you?"

"I do."

"By the way? My mom says she knew she was going to marry my dad about a week after they met." Curtis smiled. "Dad says it took him a little longer. He knew after two weeks." He speared Sam with an intense gaze. "Eleven days. Pfft." He disappeared out of the office.

Sam got up from his chair and wandered over to the large window that overlooked the backyard. *Can it really be that simple?*

Curtis's words were still in his head. *You can make this as real as you want it.*

The only difficulty with that argument was that Sam didn't think he was ready to make it as real as things could get.

"DO I look okay?" Gary asked Sam as they reached the front door of his parents' house. He'd taken an hour to decide on his clothing. The prospect of meeting Sam's family was a daunting one, and he was conscious of wanting to make a good impression.

Because if this goes how I want it to go, they're going to be my family too.

Sam snickered. "You look fine, which I've already told you at least twice, and if you didn't, it's a little late to be doing anything about it. Got your ring on?"

"Yup." Gary held up his left hand. He wished he could wear it on his ring finger, but the risk was too great. He imagined Sam would be heartbroken if he lost it.

"Then let's do this." Sam paused, finger at the doorbell. "Take a deep breath, and remember: my relatives don't bite." He pushed the bell and added, "Much."

Gary growled. "Has anyone told you lately you can be a real bitch sometimes?"

To his surprise, Sam leaned across and kissed his cheek. "Only you, honey. Only you." He grinned as the door opened.

Marshall greeted them with a hug each. "We were beginning to think you'd forgotten where we lived," he joked, leading them through the hallway toward the living room. From the sound of it, the party was already in full swing. Laughter and chatter filled the air, accompanied by the sound of piano music playing softly in the background.

"Hey, I asked Mom if she wanted us here early to help set up and she said no," Sam groused. "And just how many people have you invited?"

"Only about thirty," his dad told him. He opened the door and called out, "Look who's here!"

There was a lull in the chatter and heads turned in their direction.

"Finally!" Moira approached them, her arms wide. She kissed Gary's cheek. "Lovely to see you again. Let me introduce you to everyone."

Gary scarcely had time to glance over his shoulder and gaze plaintively at Sam before he was led away. Sam, the bastard, was grinning—until he was set upon by a clearly excited relative who flung her arms around him and nearly squashed the life out of him.

Serves him right.

"**ANYONE** seen my fiancé?" Sam asked his mom half-jokingly. He hadn't seen Gary for the last twenty minutes.

"Try the backyard," she suggested, the frown lines across her brow deepening.

Ah-ha. He's gone for a cigarette. "I'll bring him in, shall I?"

She nodded. "Your Uncle Patrick and Aunt Sarah will be leaving soon. I'm sure they'd like to say good-bye."

Sam left her putting out more canapes and went through the kitchen to the back door. He stepped outside into the cooling evening air. There was no sign of Gary near the house, and with the failing light, it was proving difficult to see much, but Sam spied him at the far end of the lawn, sitting on the bench that circled the oak tree. The thin trail of smoke was clearly visible.

Sam strolled along the path that cut through the lawn until he reached Gary, who glanced up at him and then quickly averted his gaze. "So tell me," Sam said, perching on the bench next to him. "Why are you out here, hiding?"

"It was beginning to feel like the Spanish Inquisition in there," Gary said before taking a long draw on his cigarette. He blew out the smoke and sagged against the tree trunk. "God, you have a lot of cousins."

Sam laughed. "Yes, I do. We don't get together very often—we did when I was a kid, but I guess everyone is all grown up now and life makes demands of us. It *is* rare to have so many under one roof at once." He coughed. "That might be due to us."

Gary snorted. "Yeah, I thought as much." He gestured toward the house with his cigarette. "Have you any idea how many times I've been asked when the wedding will be? I feel like making a sign and holding it above my head. It can say in bright red letters: 'No, we haven't set a date yet. Yes, you can come—*when* we set a date.'" He smiled. "Think that ought to do it?"

Sam shifted closer and took hold of Gary's hand between his. "Feeling a little overwhelmed?" He liked the intimacy of their connection. It felt… right.

"Just a little. You have all these aunts, uncles, cousins, friends of the family…. I'm not used to it." Gary chuckled. "I guess I'd better get used to it, huh? Especially if we end up getting married after all." He stubbed out the cigarette on the ground and reached into his pocket.

Sam caught the waft of peppermint and held out his hand. "I'll have one of those, if I may."

Gary handed him a stick of mint-flavored gum and Sam chewed it slowly.

"Would you mind it so much?" Sam wanted to know. "Suddenly finding yourself with a ready-made family?"

Gary smiled. "If I'm honest? It will be nice to have a family again. It just takes some getting used to. They were all telling me about what you were like as a little boy, how much trouble you used to get into."

Sam gasped in mock horror. "I was a good boy."

"Not according to your cousin Edmond." Gary snickered. "Something about a, quote, 'bag of flaming poop' on someone's doorstep?"

"Lies, all of it," Sam muttered, but he couldn't keep a straight face for long. "Oh my God. That was totally Granddad's fault. He was the one who suggested it, but I couldn't get it to work! And then Mrs. Finlay came home early and caught me."

"What happened?" Gary asked between bouts of laughing.

"Nasty old witch made me clean it up with my bare hands," he said with a groan. "Lord, I can still smell it."

"Ew!" Gary grimaced. "I've changed my mind. I don't think I want to marry you after all." They both sat there laughing, Gary leaning into his shoulder, a welcome weight. When they'd finally stopped, Gary lifted his chin to gaze directly at Sam. "Can we be spotted from the house?"

Sam took a quick look. "Not unless they have a pair of binoculars trained on us."

"Kiss me." The words had a husky edge to them. "Please?"

Like Sam could resist, with the way Gary was looking at him, his face barely lit by the solar garden lamps around them. Sam cupped his face, drawing him closer, until suddenly Gary pulled back.

"Oopsie." Hastily he removed his gum and looked around.

Sam picked up a rock from the display at his feet. "Stick it under there. She'll never know." He added his own, too, and replaced the rock back where he'd found it.

Gary was laughing quietly. "See? They're right about you."

Sam drew him close once more. "Then maybe you should be more careful. I'm obviously a bad boy."

Gary grinned. "What if I like bad boys?" he whispered and closed the distance between them.

The kiss started out chaste, but when Gary snaked a hand across Sam's chest and brushed over his nipple, Sam couldn't repress his shiver. He slid his tongue between Gary's parted lips, and the soft sound of desire that escaped made him *want*.

"Sam? Gary?"

Damn it.

They broke apart.

"Don't worry," Gary murmured against his neck. "I know where you're sleeping tonight, remember? This isn't finished." He got up from the bench and held out his hand. "We'd better go in before she sends out a search party."

Sam took his hand, his mind in a whirl.

How can I be excited, nervous, apprehensive, and horny, all at the same time?

Chapter Fourteen

First Night, First sight

I'M going to grab a quick shower before bed, if that's okay," Gary said.

The thought of Gary naked under the jets of water sent tremors coursing through Sam. He had to get out of there.

"Sure. I'm going down to the kitchen to fetch a glass of water."

Anything rather than see Gary get undressed. The nights he'd stayed at the house, Sam had only seen him in a soft blue robe.

Why does the thought of seeing him naked make me so freaking nervous?

Like he had to ask *that* question. Gary's kisses had awakened him to the thrill and anticipation of sex. And every time they kissed, all Sam could think about was the two of them....

Okay, I need to stop right there.

Mom was in the kitchen. "I thought you'd gone to bed," she said with a frown.

"Oh, I'm sorry. I didn't realize I wasn't allowed out of my room," he said dryly. That earned him a whack on the arm. "Hey, Mom? I'm not a teenager anymore. Will you stop doing that?"

"When you stop sassing me, I'll stop hitting you," she said with a sweet smile. "I take it you want something."

He went over to the cabinet and removed a glass. "Just some water." The house was quiet around them. The party had gone on until midnight, and the last guests had departed by one. Three or four relatives were staying the night, those who'd traveled the farthest to be there.

"Actually, I'm glad I've got this chance to talk to you," Mom said quietly. "Your room has everything you could need—and I do mean everything." Her cheeks pinked up.

"What are you up to?" It was rare to see her so... flustered. Mom did not "do" flustered.

"Well, I did a little shopping this week and I bought... condoms and... personal lubricant. Although the cute guy at the store called it lube." She wrinkled her nose, as if the word tasted funny in her mouth. "I put them in your nightstand." Then her eyes sparkled. "He really was cute, you know. If it wasn't for Gary, I would have introduced you."

It was official: the world had just stopped on its axis. "Excuse me? You went *shopping* for these?" He had visions of his mom in a drug store, dropping a box of Trojans into her basket. Just the image in his head was plain *wrong*. And as for her even *thinking* about trying to find him dates....

"I went online first," she said. "I found this neat little store downtown—actually, I found two of them! Right in Asheville! Anyway, I went to take a look."

"Please, tell me you didn't take Dad with you," he groaned.

"Pfft. Like I'd do that. He'd spoil all my fun." She grinned, clearly having gotten over her embarrassment. "They had so many things. I saw something I think you and Gary could have a lot of fun with. I'm going to pick it up for your birthday."

Lord, take me now. Sam did not want to even hazard a guess.

"I asked the clerk at the store for some advice, and he made a suggestion. And there were so many different lubes to choose from, but he said the one I picked was really good. He said it's water soluble, and edible, so you don't have to worry if you get some in your—"

"*Mom!*"

Her mouth snapped shut and she blinked several times in quick succession.

Sam took a deep breath. "I'm glad you went to such lengths, but you didn't have to." He stifled a groan. "You *really* didn't have to." He gave her a peck on the cheek. "I'm going to bed. We are *not* talking about this again. You got me?"

She nodded. "Good night."

He took his glass and escaped to the sanctuary of his room. Sam closed the door softly behind him and shook his head.

That did not just happen.

The bathroom door was open, but the shower wasn't running. Either Gary hadn't showered yet, or his idea of a quick shower bore no resemblance to Sam's. He could never spend less than ten minutes in a shower. Sam placed the glass on the nightstand and couldn't resist opening the drawer. He shut it hurriedly at the sight of a box of condoms and a bottle of cherry-flavored lube.

Can't think about that.

He caught the sound of humming and peered through the gap in the doorway, unable to stop himself.

Then Sam stopped breathing.

Gary had his back to the door while he rubbed himself down with a towel. Sam couldn't tear his gaze away from the curve of Gary's neck down to his shoulders, the smooth line of his nude back, down to where it swelled into a firm, round ass. *Lord, he has dimples.* Strong, lean thighs covered in a down of dark blond hair.

He's beautiful.

Then Gary bent over to dry his feet, and Sam had a perfect view of his crack, with just the merest hint of what lay hidden behind dark blond fur. He swallowed hard, but his mouth was dry.

Then it struck him. *I'm perving on him. This is so wrong.*

Quickly Sam stripped off his clothing and pulled on his sleep pants before Gary could come back into the room. He dove under the sheets and attempted to affect a calm he didn't feel.

Gary walked out of the bathroom and smiled at him. "Do you want to use the bathroom?" He wore a pair of soft-looking gray sleep pants that sat low on his hips. Sam tried not to stare at Gary's lean torso, a trail of dark blond hair disappearing under the waistband, below which was visible the outline of his dick. His erect dick.

Fuck.

Sam made a supreme effort and rolled onto his side, facing away from Gary. "I brushed my teeth before you went in there," he explained. The mattress dipped as Gary got into bed. Before he could say a word, Sam reached out and switched off the lamps. "Well, good night."

The only sound in the still room was Gary's breathing. After a moment, a chuckle came. "And good night to you too."

Sam heaved a sigh of relief and shut his eyes tight, trying not to think about the fact that he was sharing a bed for the first time ever.

Am I mad? I could just roll over and we could....

More tremors coursed through him. *No, we could not....*

Sheets rustled. The mattress dipped in the center. Soft lips brushed against Sam's ear before kissing gently down his neck, sending shivers down his spine.

"Like that?" Gary whispered.

In spite of the writhing knot of snakes in his belly, Sam couldn't deny how damn good it felt. "Yeah," he whispered, and Gary went right back to kissing his shoulder. Unhurried, like they had all the time in the world. Like they shared a bed every night and this was nothing new. He could smell Gary's shampoo, a masculine, citrus smell that infiltrated his nostrils.

When Gary slid a hand over his waist to stroke his belly, Sam wanted to moan aloud at the sensual touch. He could feel the heat from Gary's body as he shifted closer, and then suddenly there was definitely more heat pressed up against his ass. Heat and hardness.

Sam shuddered out a sigh, and Gary kissed his neck once more. He rocked slowly against Sam's ass.

"You feel that?" His voice was low and hoarse.

"Yes," Sam croaked.

When Gary slowly slid his hand lower to cup Sam's thickening shaft through his sleep pants, there was no way Sam could keep back the soft moan. Gary gave his length a gentle squeeze before stroking it. Sam grew harder at his touch, and Gary's breathing sped up.

"Oh, you definitely like that," he said with a quiet chuckle, his fingers still stroking up and down Sam's shaft. Sam pushed into his hand, and Gary's breathing grew more rapid. "I know you said you were a bad boy. You neglected to mention that you're also a big boy." He squeezed Sam through the sleep pants. "A very big boy." His fingers moved higher to edge their way under the waistband, and Sam was breathing so hard, he thought he was about to hyperventilate.

Then breathing became difficult when for the first time in his life, Sam felt another man's hand wrap around his dick.

God, that feels good.

Sam shifted onto his back, cupped Gary's head, and pulled him in for a kiss. Gary let go of Sam's cock and drew his hand up to hold Sam's face tenderly. The kisses were lingering, growing more intimate, more heated, and when Gary brought his leg over Sam's, he could feel that hard length rubbing against him. Gary's mouth was on his neck, kissing down to his collarbones.

"I guess we'll have to keep this quiet," he whispered, "seeing as your parents are in the next room." Another ripe chuckle followed his words.

And with that, Sam's passion dwindled. Gently he pushed Gary off him and reached across to switch on the lamp.

Gary blinked at him in the light. "Okay, what just happened?"

Sam rolled onto his side so he faced Gary. "I'm sorry, but there is no *way* on this planet that I want my first time to be in my parents' house."

Gary stared at him for a moment and then snorted. "Oh my God. Yeah, I can understand that." He bit back a smile. "Especially with your mom being... well, like she is."

Sam shook his head. "You have no idea." He yanked open the drawer, pulled out the condoms and lube, and dropped them onto the bed. "She went shopping for us," he said by way of explanation.

Gary stared open-mouthed. "Oh my." He picked up the lube and his eyebrows lifted. "Cherry-flavored? Really?" He smirked. "How... appropriate."

Sam gaped at him, and then he saw the funny side. Seconds later they were both laughing quietly, the bed shaking.

"Actually? Now that I know this?" Gary's shoulders shook. "Yeah, you're right. This would feel so weird." He handed the condoms and lube back to Sam. "Quick. Put them back in the drawer before I have to think about where they came from."

Sam wanted to laugh with relief. He leaned closer and kissed Gary on the mouth, really liking how Gary held him, his arms wrapped around him, their bodies pressed up against each other's.

"But just so you know?" Gary told him quietly. "This is not over. This is just a postponement." He cupped Sam's chin and kissed him lightly on the lips. "You got that, Senator?" He grinned as he pulled away.

"Got it." *Damn*, Sam sounded husky.

"Now turn out the light so we can get some sleep." Sam didn't miss the note of amusement. "That's if you can sleep in that state." The bed shook.

"This is *not* funny," Sam said with a low growl as he plunged the room into darkness once more. He rolled onto his side, facing the wall.

"Oh, I disagree." Gary shifted closer. "Besides, I'm in the same boat." His lips brushed Sam's ear, making him shudder. "You got me as hard as a rock, Sam," he whispered. "So three guesses what I'm going to be dreaming of?"

"Oh, I don't know. Cold showers? Your kindergarten teacher? Hearing my mom applaud if she thought we were going at it?"

Gary let out a gasp. "She wouldn't."

"I have three little words for you: Cherry. Flavored. Lube."

Gary sighed. "Well, that worked." He kissed Sam's shoulder before snuggling down under the sheets. "Good night." A moment later. "Sam? Would you mind if we… spooned? I'd really like to go to sleep with my arms around you."

Lord. Sam wanted that too. "Sure. Cuddle up," he said, sounding a good deal more nonchalant than he was feeling right at that moment.

The mattress undulated and then Gary had his arm around Sam's waist, his face buried in Sam's neck. The sigh that caressed Sam's skin spoke of contentment. "This is nice."

Sam couldn't agree more. He felt warm and safe. They lay there, Sam wrapped in Gary's arms, glowing in the joy of finally sharing his bed with someone.

Not *someone*: Gary. That made all the difference.

"Gary?" he murmured quietly, aware of how regular his breathing had become.

"Hmm?"

"My mom said she would set me up with a guy from the porn shop if I wasn't already getting married to you." Gary's sleepy chuckle tickled his neck, and Sam smiled to himself. "Just so you know? I'm never going to let you go now."

Another chuckle. "Fat chance, Sam. As if I'd let you. G'night, babe."

Sam lay there and listened as Gary slipped into sleep, his breathing becoming deeper. It wasn't long before it pulled him into sleep too.

Sunday night

"ARE you sure you want to keep working the phones?" Sam asked. Dinner was over and Gary was curled up on the couch, reviewing notes from the previous week's classes. "Because I'd understand if you prefer to concentrate on your studies."

Gary closed his notebook with an exaggerated sigh and placed it on the low coffee table beside the couch. "I get it. You're tired of having me around the office already. You've found someone else. You're going to marry Curtis instead." He had to duck when a cushion narrowly missed his head. "Ah-ha! I must've hit close to the mark with that last comment."

"Idiot," Sam said good-naturedly. He got up from the couch to put another log on the fire and then settled back, his eyes closed. "I love how peaceful it is here."

Gary glanced around the log cabin. "Now that I've seen your house in Asheville, I can understand why you rent this place. They both have that same tranquil quality about them."

Sam opened his eyes and stared at Gary, nodding slowly. "That's right, they do." He smiled. "I'm glad you like it here."

I like it because you're *here, Sam.* Not for the first time, Gary wished he had the nerve to tell Sam how he really felt, but as always, something held him back. It was true things had gotten more physical between them, but sleeping with Sam in his arms was a far cry from telling Sam he was falling in love with him. Gary had argued with himself long and hard about that too. He told himself it was too soon. That it couldn't be love. Lust? Yeah, maybe. There was no denying he wanted Sam. The previous night had been an eye-opener, leaving him in no doubt as to whether Sam wanted him too.

But it's more than lust. Being with Sam… completed him.

Gary had been through a couple of relationships, and at the time, he'd convinced himself this was *it*, this was love. It had taken two weeks—*two freaking weeks!*—with Sam to make those relationships pale into insignificance. He wanted this to last. He wanted the happy ending, the two of them exchanging vows to spend a lifetime together.

God, he *so* wanted this to be real.

How can he have gotten to me so fast? Gary hadn't even seen it coming. One minute he was agreeing to this… play, this *production* of Josh's, with the promise of financial solvency, and the next? He was contemplating spending the rest of his life with this beautiful man. The more he learned about Sam—his history, his family—the more Gary fell deeper in love with him. He still found it difficult to believe Sam had made it to his age without ever knowing how profound a connection sex could provide.

Then show him. Rock his freaking world.

Gary liked that idea. Liked it a whole lot.

"Hey, Sam?" Gary moved along the couch until he was sitting next to Sam, their thighs touching.

Sam stared at him, his lips parted. No sound came forth, but his chest rose and fell a little more rapidly.

Gary leaned over and put his hand on Sam's nape and drew him closer until their lips met, tentatively at first on Sam's part, but quickly becoming more confident. Gary didn't keep their kisses chaste for long. He yearned for Sam to see how much Gary wanted him, how much he needed him. He stroked his tongue between Sam's lips and was rewarded with a soft, low noise that spoke of Sam's own need.

Gary paused his kisses long enough to unbutton Sam's shirt, Sam watching his fingers as they freed the top three buttons. Gary kissed him again, slow and deliberate, while he eased his hand beneath the fabric to caress Sam's chest, with its covering of dark brown hair. The noise Sam made at the back of his throat and the way he deepened the kiss told Gary all he needed to know.

He wants this too.

Another button was undone so Gary could move his hand over Sam's bare shoulder under the shirt before stroking up his neck, rubbing his thumb along

Sam's jaw. Gary eased his arm behind Sam's head to support him while he caressed and stroked, flicking Sam's nipple and listening to the hitch in his breathing. When Gary pulled Sam's shirt free of his pants to undo the last few buttons, this time Sam was helping him.

"Take it off, babe." Gary sounded hoarse to his own ears.

Sam nodded, his gaze focused on Gary's face while he sat up and freed his arms. Gary pulled the shirt off him and dropped it to the floor. One glance at Sam's crotch was enough to tell him where this was leading. Gary couldn't resist. He slid his hand down over Sam's taut belly and gently squeezed his erection. Sam's breathing changed. Short, hoarse breaths filled the air as Sam unfastened his belt, his hand trembling. Gary placed his hand over Sam's and kissed him until the tremors subsided.

"There's no hurry," he whispered. "We're going to take this nice and slow."

Sam swallowed. "We… we're not going to stop tonight, are we?"

Gary smiled. "No, Sam. Not tonight. So how about we take this to the bedroom?" The smile became a grin. "Because believe me, much as I like your charmingly rustic floor? I do *not* want splinters in my ass."

Sam bit back a smirk. "You may have a point."

"Yeah, and that's exactly what I'm talking about. Sharp points that make their way into knees and asses." He got up off the couch and held out his hand. "Let's go make love."

Slowly Sam rose to his feet, the firelight playing over his bare skin. He nodded, and without a word, Gary led him into Sam's bedroom.

Chapter Fifteen

Handing in the V card

SAM'S heart pounded as Gary led him by the hand to the bed.

It's finally going to happen. Except that he no longer saw what was coming as losing his virginity. It was simply time to know *all* of Gary, to see him as he'd never seen him before—and for Sam to allow someone to see all of himself.

Gary paused at the side of the bed. "Now is a good time to ask if we have supplies." The slightly breathless quality in his voice told Sam that Gary wasn't as calm as he appeared. The thought comforted him.

Sam had to smile at his words. "Maybe we should have brought some of Mom's 'purchases' with us."

Gary flushed and let go of his hand. He disappeared through the door to his own room and returned a moment later with the box of Trojans—and a different bottle of lube. "I 'liberated' these from the nightstand while you were showering this morning," he confessed. He held up the bottle. "This is mine. I'm sorry, but I draw the line at cherry-flavored lube," he said with a wry smile. When Sam lifted his eyebrows, Gary's flush deepened. "I never could stand those artificial flavors," he muttered.

The laughter that bubbled up and out of Sam felt right. "Good to know."

Gary dropped the items on the bed and slowly walked around to where Sam stood. "Now, where were we?"

"We were kissing. Hopefully we're going to have more of that," Sam murmured.

Gary's smile lit up his face. "I love it when we're on the same page." He inclined his head. "Now how about we both lie down on the same bed?" He pushed Sam's shoulders until he was sitting on the edge of the mattress, and then Gary joined him, pulling him gently until they were lying in the center, Sam on his back, Gary on his side leaning over him.

Sam reached up and curved his hands around Gary's head, drawing him down into a kiss.

Lord, Gary could kiss.

Gary's hand was on his neck, soft and gentle, his thumb rubbing along Sam's jaw while he kissed Sam so slowly, as if he was trying to imprint the taste and feel of Sam onto his memory. There was no urgency, just this slow burn that sent warmth spreading throughout Sam's body. Sam lost himself in Gary's kisses, in the feel of Gary's T-shirt, soft against Sam's bare skin, in the noises of delight Gary made as he deepened their kisses.

Sam couldn't help but respond. He fused their mouths together in a kiss that sent tingles all over his body. Gary stroked down over his chest, moving at a leisurely pace that kept time with their kisses. His fingers skated over Sam's belly, light and playful, and Sam shivered at the touch. But when Gary reached his opened belt, Sam caught his breath.

Gary's eyes met his. "Take it off for me."

The throaty request sent blood heading south, and Sam's dick gave a throb behind the zipper of his pants. He let go of Gary and attempted to remove the belt, his damn fingers not cooperating.

Gary smiled and helped him, slowly pulling the belt free of its loops and tossing it to the foot of the bed. "Like I said, we're going to take it nice and slow." He caressed Sam's shaft through his pants, squeezing it and feeling its length. Gary gave a gasp. "Whoa. What have you got in there—an anaconda?"

Sam looked down and gave a nervous chuckle. "Damn. You spoiled my surprise." But all thoughts of laughter left him in a hurry when Gary lowered the zipper, slipped his hand inside, and rubbed over his briefs. "God, yes," he breathed.

Gary paused. "I think we're wearing far too many clothes." Before Sam could react, Gary knelt up, grabbed hold of his pants, and pulled them past Sam's hips. He moved to Sam's feet, where he tugged at the pants until Sam was lying there in nothing but a pair of black briefs clinging to his erect dick, which pushed at the fabric. Gary took his time removing his own T-shirt and jeans, revealing a pair of tight white briefs that struggled to contain his cock.

"Do you like what you see?"

Sam's throat tightened and his mouth dried up. "Yes." The whispered syllable was all he could manage. He cleared his throat and swallowed. "Gary, you're… you're beautiful."

Gary's lips parted and his breathing hitched. "Oh. Thank you." He smiled. "No more beautiful than the man I'm looking at."

Then he was stretched out beside Sam once more, rolling Sam onto his side and pulling him into his arms. Their bodies connected from their chests down to their knees. Gary kissed him, still taking his time, only now his hands stroked gently over Sam's skin, skimming his waist and reaching lower to squeeze his ass. Sam let out a low moan, and Gary broke the kiss to stare into Sam's eyes. "Sam, for God's sake, touch me," he groaned.

Hesitantly, Sam placed his hand on Gary's bare skin and slowly, so slowly, caressed him, his fingertips learning the feel of him. Sam closed his eyes and breathed Gary in, the warm, clean smell of him.

Gary let out a sigh of pleasure. "Oh, that's nice. You have a sensual touch." A gentle hand pressed against his cheek. "Hey. Look at me."

Sam opened his eyes and Gary smiled.

"You have good hands, Senator." He covered one of Sam's hands with his own and slowly guided it lower, over his hip, down to his swollen dick, the cotton molding around it. "Touch me, Sam," he whispered.

Sam cupped Gary's erection and Gary pushed into his palm, his breathing speeding up a little. Sam stroked him through his briefs, not daring to go further—until Gary stopped his gentle movement.

"Look," he said quietly.

Sam glanced down, and Gary pulled the waistband away from his skin to reveal his hard cock.

"See that? You make me so hard, Sam." He pulled his dick free of his briefs, and Sam stared at it, the thick shaft, the wide head, a drop of precome already beading there....

"Please?"

Sam didn't miss the edge to Gary's voice. For the first time in his life, he wrapped his hand around an erect dick that wasn't his own. *Lord*, it was hot, the skin like silk, but hard like steel beneath it. Sam stroked up and down its length, and Gary shuddered.

"I've wanted to feel that for a while now." He leaned in and kissed Sam, moaning softly into his mouth when Sam began to pull gently at his cock, venturing lower to touch the delicate skin covering his balls with hesitant fingers. "God, yes. That's so good."

His words lit a fire inside Sam's belly. Sam stroked and caressed, squeezing, learning the feel of him, loving it when Gary's breath caught in his throat, when he shivered at Sam's touch.

This was Gary 101.

Gary buried his face in Sam's neck, kissing him there, moving lower until his lips were around Sam's nipple, and Sam couldn't stop his hips from moving. He let go of Gary's dick and shuddered as Gary tugged gently, his nipple caught between Gary's teeth. Then Gary was kissing him again, only this time his hand was busy removing Sam's underwear.

Oh Lord.

Sam groaned into the kiss and lifted up to aid Gary. A whisper of fabric against skin, a similar sound as Gary took off his own briefs—and Sam lay naked on the bed, an equally naked Gary pressed up against him.

Gary gazed down at their bodies and his eyes widened. "Oh my." A shudder rippled its way down the length of Sam's body when Gary slowly stroked his dick, curling his fingers around the base, squeezing the wide shaft.

Sam pushed up with his hips, wanting more.

Gary smiled. "Patience."

Sam wasn't sure he had any left in him. Every nerve ending in his body appeared to have burst into life and was clamoring for more.

Gary rolled them both until he was astride Sam, his dick hot and hard against Sam's belly. He shoved pillows behind Sam's head and went right back to kissing, like he needed kisses to breathe. Sam exulted in the feel of skin on skin, the warmth of their bodies, the way Gary undulated his hips in a slow wave while he claimed Sam's mouth.

Gary paused midkiss to whisper against Sam's lips. "You have an addictive mouth, do you know that?" Then before Sam could take a breath, Gary went right back to kissing him.

Sam wound his arms around Gary's body and held him close, loving that feeling of connection between them, of lips, skin, hands, tongues....

He wasn't the only one with an addictive mouth.

Gary sat up, took hold of Sam's hands, and pulled them gently but insistently around to where Gary's ass met Sam's groin. He pressed them against the firm globes and smiled. "Touch. Explore. Discover."

In spite of his excited state, Sam couldn't help grinning. "And what will I discover?" He squeezed Gary's ass before edging his fingers closer to his crease. Gary bit his lip, shifted forward, and tilted his hips, pushing back into Sam's touch. Sam slid a single finger between his cheeks and stifled a moan when he rubbed over Gary's entrance, the skin so hot there. Sam shivered, a dark frisson skating up and down his back. This was new, intimate, sensual....

It was damn hot.

Gary nodded, his gaze locked on Sam's. "Looks like you found something." His voice was husky with desire.

The sensation blossoming in Sam's belly felt *huge*, and an urgent need raced through him. "Kiss me?"

Gary didn't hesitate. He stretched out on top of Sam, and their mouths met once more, Sam losing himself in their kisses. Only now there was an edge to them, something that spoke of Gary's hunger, his need.

Anticipation bubbled inside Sam until he wanted to cry out with it, his desire white-hot.

Gary kissed his way down Sam's chest, pausing briefly to renew his acquaintance with his nipples before kissing lower, tracing Sam's abs with his tongue. Sam couldn't tear his gaze away from the sight of Gary worshipping his body with lips, tongue, and fingers. He could feel the heat from Gary's dick as Gary shifted position—and *holy hell*, Gary was pushing a knee between his, nudging, encouraging Sam to spread for him. His heart pounding, Sam gave him access, and Gary was lying between his legs, his face inches above Sam's groin where his cock was already rising to greet Gary. Sam's pulse raced and breathing became a chore.

Gary lifted his head to meet Sam's gaze and then all the air left Sam's lungs in a long exhale when Gary's lips met the head of his cock. *Shit. How could I ever have thought those eyes were cool?* The look Gary was giving him was hot enough to melt glass. And *oh my*

God, the way that mouth felt around his dick. Wet heat surrounded it, sucking him deeper, the friction of those lips around his shaft just perfect.

If Sam had thought his cock was hard before....

"I had... no idea," Sam moaned. He wanted to move, to thrust up into that hot mouth. He wound his fingers through the longish hair on top of Gary's head and held him there while he carefully rocked his hips, pushing a little deeper. Gary groaned in approval, and, encouraged, Sam began to move a bit faster, unable to take his eyes off his slick cock as it slid in and out of Gary's mouth. Lord, it was all so *wonderful*: the feel of Gary's tongue as it played over his shaft; the delicious suction when Gary took him deeper still; the sounds Gary made around his length; and the sound of his own breathing, harsh and staccato, his hunger growing by the second.

Then everything came to a halt.

Unhurried, Gary knelt up and shifted position until he was straddling Sam's chest, his legs spread wide. His dick was rigid, pointing at Sam, thick and tempting. Gary's hot gaze was locked on his face. "Sam? Do you want to...?"

Sam didn't wait to hear the rest of the question. He lifted his head from the pillows and licked the head of Gary's cock before sliding his tongue along the underside.

"Oh God, yeah, just like that," Gary gasped. "Wrap your lips over your teeth and suck me." He grabbed the back of Sam's head, supporting him and pushing gently between his lips. Sam slid his mouth along Gary's shaft, moving slowly back and forth. He could feel every ridge, every indentation. When Gary's dick throbbed in his mouth, Sam lost himself in the sensation of hot, hard flesh on his tongue.

It was like a piece of him that had always been missing finally clicked into place.

With a shudder Gary pulled free of him. "Oh my God, you got me so close," he said breathlessly. "And tempting though the idea is of coming into your mouth, I want to wait until you're inside me."

That sent a shockwave through Sam. *Inside him.* He was surprised he didn't come then and there.

Gary was regarding him with shining eyes. "You like that idea." It wasn't a question. He sat there, his cock pointing heavenward, his chest flushed. "I'm going to need your fingers," he said with a wicked smile.

Something deep inside Sam's belly rolled over, and the image in his head sent icy shivers up and down his spine.

Gary reached across the bed for the bottle of lube. "You need to prepare me, babe." He took Sam's hand and squirted drops of the clear, thick liquid onto his fingers. Once he'd put the bottle aside, Gary wrapped his hand around Sam's wrist and guided him through his spread legs. "Slowly push a finger inside me. And I do mean slowly." He smiled. "It's been a while, all right?"

Sam did as instructed, his heartbeat racing. He took infinite care not to move too quickly or too deep—the last thing he wanted was to cause Gary any discomfort. But one glance at the expression on Gary's face when Sam finally sank a finger into him was enough to reassure him.

"Damn, I'd forgotten how good it feels when it's not me doing that." Gary sighed. He closed his eyes and began to slowly rock on Sam's finger, taking it deeper.

Sam was amazed at the heat and tightness inside him. When Gary begged for another finger, Sam was filled with a savage pride. And when Gary began to ride his fingers hard, Sam felt like his heart was about to burst.

"Sam, you gotta stop," Gary said with a gasp.

Sam froze. "What… what did I do wrong?"

Gary laughed and bent down to kiss him. "Absolutely nothing, babe. You're too good at this. You've got me right on the edge. I feel like the second you're inside me, I'll come." He cupped Sam's cheek tenderly. "And I want your first time to last a little longer than ten seconds, okay?"

Sam snorted. "What makes you think I'll last *that* long?"

"Next time we go shopping, I'm taking you to that store your mom found and we're going to buy you a cock ring," Gary said with a wicked glint in his eye. He grabbed the box of condoms and removed one. "We can't have you coming too soon. Ah well. This is what I get for dating an older guy." He bit his lip. "At least I should be thankful you can still get it up at your age."

Sam knew the wisecracks for what they were, an attempt to assuage his nerves, and his heart swelled. The words were right there, on the tip of his tongue. *God, I love you.*

He held his dick steady around the base. "Come on, honey. I want to make love to you."

Gary's face glowed. "I want that too," he whispered. He tore open the packet and unrolled the condom over Sam's heavy cock, then grabbed the lube to make it nice and slick. Gary lay on his back, his arms wide. "Come here, you."

Sam shifted carefully until he was on all fours above him, Gary's legs spread wide.

Gary curled a hand around Sam's neck. "Kiss me. I want you to kiss me while you're entering me."

His words had Sam's heart pounding like never before.

Sam bent low and kissed him, exploring him leisurely with his tongue while he guided his slippery cock into position. He could feel Gary's heat against the head.

"Now, Sam, please."

Sam took a deep breath and pushed, sinking slowly into Gary while they kissed, tongues sliding between parted lips, each of them feeding sighs into the other's mouth as Sam inched his dick into Gary's body. Gary fed him a deep groan and looped his arms around Sam's neck. Their foreheads touched, and Sam began to move, carefully at first, overwhelmed by the heat of him. It was exquisite, the two of them rocking together, moving as one.

"God, how you feel," Sam gasped. "So tight around me."

"Sam… please…." Gary looked up into his eyes. "I need…."

Sam kept his gaze fixed on those gorgeous green eyes. "I know, baby." He started to pick up speed. *Lord*, the temptation to thrust deep and hard into Gary was enormous, but he quashed his own hunger. He wanted it to be good for *both* of them. "This what you need? Faster?"

Gary's hands were on his back, his shoulders, fingers digging into him, his breathing quickening. "Slow and deep," he said, his eyes wide.

Sam complied, filling him to the hilt. "Like that?" Sam asked, watching Gary's face as he slid into him, feeling Gary's body ripple around his dick.

Gary moaned, fingers clutching at Sam, his legs crossing at the ankles at Sam's lower back. "God, yes, that's perfect." Gary pulled him down hard into a kiss that was all lips and tongue, and Sam went willingly, hips rolling as he fought to maintain his rhythm. Gary let go of him and pulled his knees up toward his chest, changing the angle, and suddenly Sam was deeper than ever.

"You feel amazing," he growled, plunging his cock into Gary's tight channel. "I'm so close."

"Me too—oh *fuck*, there! Again!" Gary's body was writhing on his dick, almost dancing on it, moving to meet his thrusts. "Now, Sam, go hard *now*. Fuck me," he pleaded.

Sam groaned and pushed all the way into him, hips rocking faster. He propped himself up on his arms and pistoned into Gary, his balls drawing up high and tight. He couldn't stave off his climax any longer. "God, Gary, gonna…." Then he was crying out, overtaken by the sheer bliss of coming inside Gary, shooting while deep inside him, overwhelmed by the sensation of tightness, the feeling of Gary's ass gripping his cock like a vise.

Gary shivered beneath him, body jerking as his dick erupted, covering both of them with drops of come. "Oh God, that's… oh love…."

That one word sent Sam's heartbeat into overdrive. He covered Gary with his body and took his mouth once more in a long, searing kiss, one that threatened to consume him with its heat and reduce him to a pile of ash. An off-the-scale kiss.

An *I-love-you* kiss.

Sam had to know.

He lay on top of Gary, their bodies jolting every now and then as their mutual orgasms receded, Sam still inside, still connected. He held that sweet face in his hand. "What you said just now…." He couldn't get the words out, fear thickening in his throat in case he had it all wrong.

"Huh?" Gary gazed at him with glazed eyes, lids heavy, his breathing erratic. "What did I say?"

Shit. Sam didn't dare. This was his *heart*, damn it. "Nothing," he said, forcing calm into his voice. "It was nothing." Slowly he eased out of Gary's body, holding on to the condom.

Gary's brow furrowed. "I don't understand." Then his eyes widened once again. "Oh. That." He swallowed. "Oh," he repeated.

"It's okay," Sam said gently. "I mean, we both got carried away, obviously. I—" He turned his head away, heart aching, and dealt with the condom.

"Sam? Sam, look at me."

He pushed down hard on his hopes, turned, and met Gary's gaze. "Yes?"

Gary smiled up at him, a look of utter contentment on his face. "I love you," he said simply.

Heat radiated through Sam's chest. He felt feather-light, every molecule in his body zinging into life. *Did he just say…?* "You… love me?"

Gary grinned. "Is this something else I should be aware of once we're married? Hearing loss?" He shook his head, his eyes bright. "Your mom has the right idea, you know. I should trade you in for a younger model." He bit back a smirk.

Sam growled and rolled them until Gary was on top, his face inches from Sam's. "There will be no trading in. You marry me, you're stuck with me."

Gary's expression softened. "How do the words go? 'As long as we both shall live'?"

"And beyond." Sam reached up and held Gary's face between his hands. "I… I love you too."

A sigh shuddered out of Gary. "Thank God for that." He beamed at Sam. "Now kiss me again, Senator."

"With pleasure."

Chapter Sixteen

Wednesday

"I DON'T want to get up," Sam murmured, his face buried in Gary's neck. The bed was warm, but Gary was even warmer in Sam's arms, his leg hooked over Gary's thigh.

Gary's chuckle reverberated through him. "You said the same thing yesterday. And Monday." Gary stroked down his back, a gentle caress that made Sam want to sigh with happiness. "And besides, this bed is seeing way too much action."

Sam lifted his head to look Gary in the eye. "Is that a complaint?"

Gary rolled his eyes. "As if I'd complain about that. But let's face it. We come through that front door and Sam's little head takes over. We barely make it out of the bed to cook dinner." He tugged Sam until he was lying on top of Gary, legs parting to wrap around him. "You, Senator, are insatiable."

Sam couldn't hold back his grin. "Maybe I'm just making up for lost time. Ever think of that?" He kissed Gary's throat, loving how Gary gave up a soft sigh and closed his eyes, pushing his head back into the pillows, revealing more of his neck for Sam to kiss and nibble and suck…. "God, you're addictive," Sam whispered into his ear. "Can't get enough of you." When he finally came up for air, he found Gary's gaze focused on him, his expression thoughtful.

"Should I be concerned here? Maybe I'm not enough for your… appetite?"

The words were uttered lightly enough and in a humorous tone, but Sam caught… something.

He rolled onto his side, taking Gary with him, Sam's arms around him. Sam stared into that beautiful face. "There will only ever be you," he said simply, locking gazes with Gary, hoping to God he could read how sincere Sam was being, because damn it, he meant every word.

Gary swallowed. "Sam, I… I don't doubt your veracity, not for a second, but, babe, we've been together such a short while, and in fairly unconventional circumstances. This… this is still all new to you. How can you know how you'll feel a month from now, maybe a year?" His green eyes were troubled. "I know you mean what you say, but… how can you know that?"

Sam cupped his cheek. "How can any of us know that? You're just going to have to trust me, trust what I'm telling you." He didn't break eye contact. "I don't want anyone else. I'm not about to go looking for anyone else to bring into our lives. As far as I'm concerned, you, Mr. Mason, are it. Pure and simple. For the rest of my life." He smiled. "Think you can handle that?"

Oh my God, the way he's looking at me. Sam could *see* it, see the love shining right out of him, impossible to miss.

"Oh yeah," Gary said softly. "I think I'm up to the task." He smiled. "You think anyone will notice if we're a little late this morning?"

Now Sam was grinning. "So what if they do? I'm the boss, right?"

Gary pulled the sheet up over their heads, cocooning them in it. "Yes, sir," he whispered.

SAM switched off the engine. *Mission accomplished.* He couldn't wait for Sunday. Josh had found him a really romantic restaurant for Valentine's. Of course, he'd also wanted a photographer to be there while Sam and Gary had dinner, and Sam had shot *that* idea down in flames pretty damn quick. In the end they'd agreed on a compromise: photographs before they went into the restaurant, but the photographer did *not* get to cross the threshold.

Sam got out of the car and walked into the house. He couldn't resist peeking into the phones room. Gary was only working there for another hour or so before classes. Sam spied him talking animatedly and taking notes at the same time. The other telemarketers smiled at him and waved. Sam caught Gary's eye and pointed upstairs before making a gesture he knew his fiancé would get. *Coffee.*

Gary grinned and nodded enthusiastically.

Sam went up the stairs and into his office.

"Where have you been?"

One look at Josh was enough to know something was up. He'd been running his fingers through his short, gelled hair until it was standing up in spikes. Not that his tone wasn't enough of a giveaway either.

"Do we have a problem?" Sam asked calmly while he hung his coat on a hanger. He was used to Josh's outbursts and excitable nature. "Becky? Any coffee going?"

Curtis entered the office behind him and shut the door. "You picked a fine time to go on an 'errand,'" he said quietly. "Meanwhile, *here*, the shit has well and truly hit the fan."

Josh groaned. "And then some."

Sam sat at his desk. "Okay, stop talking in riddles and tell me what's going on."

Curtis pulled up a chair. "Can I remind you again not to turn off your phone? We've been trying to reach you for an hour."

"Sorry about that," Sam said sincerely. "I had something to do and I didn't want to be disturbed."

The outer door opened and Gary came in. "Your timing is excellent. I was *so* ready for a coffee break." He walked around the desk and kissed Sam on the cheek. "Hi, babe. Did you get done whatever it was you had to do in town?"

"Look, save it for the cameras," Josh said abruptly. "And maybe after this, the pair of you need to work on your acting skills." He sank into an empty chair and stared gloomily at his phone.

Gary frowned. "Have I missed something?"

"Apparently we both have," Sam commented dryly, although he was starting to get a bad feeling in the pit of his stomach. "I'm still waiting for someone to clue us in."

Becky appeared with a tray of coffee mugs. "Have you told him yet?" she asked Curtis, her lips pursed.

Curtis opened his mouth, but Sam had had enough.

"Well, I wish *someone* would," he growled. "Becky, hand out the mugs and then take a seat. You obviously know what's going on around here."

Silence fell. Becky gave him a startled glance before following his instructions. She sat down quickly.

Josh huffed out a heavy sigh. "Barry Donovan happened, that's what. We've been found out."

"Go on." Sam forced himself to stay calm.

"Isn't he that reporter from the press conference?" Gary asked. "The one who asked Sam to kiss me?" He pulled up another chair and sat next to Sam.

Josh nodded. "It seems our intrepid Mr. Donovan has been doing a little investigating."

"Donovan has a blog," Curtis explained, "and an hour ago, he put out a post. A rather long, detailed post—about you two."

"And since then, I've sat there watching your ratings plummet. The post already has more than two hundred comments, all pretty much in the same vein."

"Josh," Sam said gently. "What did Donovan say?"

There was a moment's silence before Josh plunged ahead. "As far as I can tell, he went to every bar, every restaurant, and every store he could think of in Raleigh and flashed your pictures. Then he did the same thing in Asheville. *Then* he went to Gary's college, asking questions. He even paid a visit to your store, Sam. Apparently, it's all he's been doing ever since the press conference. And the conclusion he came to was that the good people of North Carolina were being sold a crock of shit. He said you weren't a couple, that not one person had seen the two of you together before that press conference. He said the whole thing was a scam, a fake, made up for the cameras. He said—"

"Basically he's saying we've lied," Curtis said, interrupting him. "There will be no wedding. There was no engagement. It's all a big fat lie, perpetrated so you could save face about being outed."

"I see." Sam was amazed at how calm he was taking it all.

"You see? You *see*?" Josh gaped at him. "We need to discuss damage control, like, *now*. And so much for all those photos, interviews, and articles. Ever since he broke this, I've been watching the comments. People *believe* this guy, Sam."

"It's fine." Sam regarded him frankly.

Josh's jaw dropped and his eyes widened. "Fine?"

Curtis tilted his head to one side. "I know that look. You have a plan, don't you?"

Sam smiled. "Oh yes." He turned to Josh. "Okay, I need you to organize a press conference for today. I have some calls to make, so try to give me a few hours."

"A press conference," Josh repeated. "Today."

"Yes, Josh, today."

"Is there anything I can do?" Gary asked.

Sam's heartbeat raced. It wasn't exactly what he'd planned, but…. *Fuck it.*

"Yes, actually there is." Sam got up from his chair and went over to where his coat was hanging. He reached into the inside pocket for the small box he'd left there. He slipped it into the pocket of his pants and slowly walked to where Gary was sitting, biting at his lip.

Sam gazed at him. "You can answer a question for me. I was going to ask you this Sunday over dinner, but you know what? I don't want to wait another second." And with that he got down on one knee beside Gary's chair.

The sound of four people catching their breath was electric.

"Sam, what are you doing?" Gary stared at him, his eyes wide.

"Doing things properly." Sam pulled out the small velvet box and opened it. He took out his grandfather's ring. "Gary Mason, will you do me the honor of becoming my husband?"

Gary's mouth fell open. "For... for real?"

Sam nodded. "For real, honey. I love you, and I don't want to spend another day without you at my side. Marry me, Gary?"

Gary said nothing, but leaned forward and took Sam's face between his hands. He looked directly into Sam's eyes and smiled before kissing Sam on the lips.

Lord, it had to be the sweetest kiss they'd ever shared.

When they parted, Gary regarded him with glistening eyes. "Yes, Sam. I'll marry you." He brought their foreheads together and closed his eyes. "I love you too," he whispered.

Sam took Gary's left hand in his and slid the ring onto his third finger.

Gary opened his eyes and gasped. "It fits."

Sam couldn't resist. "Why yes, it does, *Cinderfella*. I had it resized." He caught Curtis's snicker from behind him. "That was where I've just been, collecting it from the jewelers."

"But I thought... I mean, you said...." Gary seemed genuinely lost for words.

"This ring means a lot to me," Sam said quietly. "It's one of my most treasured possessions. It belonged to a man I loved dearly, so it's fitting that it's now worn by the man I love."

Gary cupped the nape of Sam's neck and pulled him into a kiss, their lips pressed together, the connection between them solid once more.

Sam didn't want to move, as if it would somehow break the spell.

Becky's loud sniff did that.

Gary pulled away, and Sam turned to look at her. She was staring at them both, tears trickling down her cheeks.

"That was the most beautiful thing I ever saw and heard."

Sam got up, Gary helping him to his feet, and Sam enveloped him in a tight hug. Lightness suffused his whole body, and he was so happy, he could have shouted it from the rooftops.

"You sneaky pair." Both Sam and Gary turned to look at Curtis, who stood there, hands on his hips. "You went and fell in love, didn't you?"

Sam grinned. "See, I *knew* there was a reason I made you my chief of staff. You're observant." He caught Curtis's warm glance of approval.

Becky cleared her throat and held out her hand.

Josh grumbled but reached into his pocket, took out his wallet, and handed Becky fifty dollars.

"What's that for?" Sam asked.

"I told him it was becoming more than what it started out to be," Becky said. "I could see it in your eyes. Josh told me I was seeing things, so we bet." She waved the money at Josh. "Pfft. Seeing things, my ass.

If I couldn't see that one coming, I deserve to hand in my badge as the president of Fag Hags Anonymous."

Gary almost choked with laughter.

"Oh my God. Boss, you *have* to let me help plan the wedding," Josh exclaimed.

"Get in line, pipsqueak," Becky growled. "This was *my* idea in the first place, remember?"

Sam laughed, and Gary and Curtis joined in.

"I vote we leave these two to fight it out," Sam suggested. "Curtis, your office? I need to make some calls, and I don't want to interrupt the Battle of the Wedding Planners here. And besides, I need your advice."

"Be my guest." Curtis opened the door.

"Don't forget, you have a press conference to arrange, Josh," Sam called out as they left the room.

The last thing Sam caught was Becky's taunt. "Oh yeah? Well, wait till you hear *my* idea for a flower girl!"

He closed the door on the two of them and glanced at Gary. "You sure you know what you're getting yourself into?"

Gary smiled and kissed his cheek. "I'm a big boy. I'll cope. Now, suppose you tell *me* what you've got planned. I mean, it *is* my wedding too, right?"

Sam gave him a sweet smile. "You'll just have to trust me."

Gary's groan was music to his ears.

"READY?" Sam asked Gary as they paused at the door to the pressroom.

Like he needed to ask. Gary's calm expression said it better than words.

Gary smiled. "Let's do this."

Curtis cleared his throat. "And here we go." He opened the door, and they walked into a frenzy of camera flashes and loud voices. Sam led Gary to their chairs and waited for Josh to get all the assembled reporters and newspeople settled. Every seat was taken, and there was no space left at the sides or at the back of the room.

Barry Donovan sat in the middle of the front row, looking smug and talking with those around him. He caught Sam's glance and gave him an evil smile.

Sam gave him what he hoped was a supremely confident smile in return. Judging by Barry's brief start, he did a good job. The reporter appeared confused by Sam's reaction, which was fine by Sam.

Let the games begin.

When he had everyone quiet, Josh picked up the handheld microphone. "Ladies and gentlemen, thank you for attending this conference at such short notice. I'm sure I don't need to mention why we're here."

"Yeah, you got busted!" Barry called out, folding his arms across his chest, apparently recovered from his earlier confusion.

Josh ignored him. "Senator Dalton has a statement to make, and after that, he will take questions from the floor. We ask that you please refrain from interrupting until he's finished. Thank you." He stepped aside and took his place next to Curtis on the sideline.

Sam glanced at Gary, who gave him a nod and a smile. Sam took the mic from its stand and rose to his feet. He gazed at the assembled crowd before him, their expectant faces focused on him, and took a deep breath.

"Ladies and gentlemen, Barry Donovan would have you believe I'm not about to get married any day soon. He would have you believe Gary Mason and I are not engaged. He would like you to believe that we're not a couple, that it's all a hoax, a publicity stunt. So I am here today with an invitation." He lifted his chin and slowly swept his gaze around the room. "It's for all of you." A buzz started up at the front of the room and rippled its way through the crowd.

In the front row, Barry stared at Sam, clearly discomforted.

Sam smiled. "You are invited to attend the wedding of Senator Samuel Dalton and Mr. Gary Mason on April 29th on the front lawn of the Biltmore Estate—weather permitting, of course," he added with a wink. "After the ceremony, you're invited to join our family, friends, and staff in toasting our future happiness with a glass of champagne. We look forward to seeing as many of you who are able to attend."

The camera flashes started up again, and the buzz of voices grew louder.

Sam held up his hand for quiet. When a hush fell, he looked directly at Barry Donovan. "As for Barry's other claims that Gary and I are not a, quote, 'real couple,' I have something else to add." He turned to Gary and held out his hand. Gary took it and stood up beside him. Sam put his arm around Gary's waist. "This is the man I love, whom I intend to make my husband. I would not entertain doing that for the sake of a publicity stunt."

The room was suddenly very quiet.

From the side, he caught Curtis's slow nod of approval.

Sam faced his audience. "I come from very traditional stock. My grandparents were married for sixty years. My parents have been married thirty-five years last weekend. Marriage is not something I take lightly, and it is *definitely* not something to be undertaken on a whim. I believe in the sanctity of marriage, and when I make my vows to Gary, in the sight of God, it will be with one clear thought in mind." He turned his head to regard Gary, his heart swelling. "That we are going to spend the rest of our lives together."

Gary was so still beside him, his focus on Sam.

Sam turned back to stare intently at Barry. "You asked me at my last press conference to kiss Gary, and I shot you down. I told you it wasn't appropriate." He smiled. "Well, it is now."

And with that he took Gary in his arms and kissed him on the mouth. Gary put his arms around him and held on to him, Sam's hand on Gary's cheek. He didn't bother keeping it chaste for the cameras. He kissed Gary slowly, as if it were only the two of them there and they weren't standing in front of a packed room of reporters who began cheering and hollering, their noise filling the air. Camera flashed, more voices were raised in approval, and still Sam kissed Gary, lost in the moment.

When they finally parted, Gary stared at him, eyes sparkling. *I love you*, he mouthed.

"I love you too," Sam whispered. He inclined his head toward their audience. "Have they finished yet?"

Gary opened his eyes wide. "There's someone else here?" Those near the front laughed.

Sam chuckled. "Unfortunately, yes. You think we'd better take some questions now?"

"Fine. As long as no one asks which of us will be wearing the dress."

Sam grinned. "Of course not. Because we both know it will be you."

If the look Gary gave him was anything to go by, Sam would be paying for that remark all night long.

Epilogue

"SAM, for God's sake, leave that tie alone. It looks fine."

Sam peered at his reflection. "You sure it's not crooked?"

Gary laughed softly and inserted himself between Sam and the full-length mirror. "Will you just trust me? You look wonderful. Elegant." He leaned closer. "Sexy as all hell."

"Down, boy," Sam said. He tried to look around Gary. "Well, if you're sure."

Gary sighed. "Senator Dalton, you look amazing." He smoothed his hand down Sam's arm. "And this suit looks awesome on you."

Sam smiled. "I took one look at you when you tried this on, and you looked so gorgeous, I knew I had to have the same one."

They both wore tuxedos in a slate gray, with white dress shirts and white bow ties. Gary had at one point considered wearing a lighter color. The thought made Sam snicker.

"What are you thinking about?" Gary asked.

"I was remembering Becky's comment at the fitting."

She'd insisted on coming with them when they went to choose their wedding suits. She'd taken one look at them and groaned. "Look, the pair of you are going to look gorgeous. So just wear the same goddamn color and let's get out of here, all right?"

"Speaking of Becky…." Gary tilted his head. "Was it her idea to put the same bow tie on our flower girl? Er, boy. Flower dog." He shrugged. "Whatever."

Sam snorted. "Who else? Although when she first suggested the idea of making Dinky part of the ceremony, I really considered having her carted off to the funny farm."

Gary grinned. "Like you didn't want that too." He kissed Sam on the tip of his nose. "You adore that dog just as much as I do."

Adopting Dinky had been Gary's idea, and Sam would have done anything to make his future husband happy. Even though that had meant asking his landlord to give them permission to keep the dog at the cabin.

"Well, true, but *flower dog*?"

"Aw, but he looks so *cute*—a matching bow tie, a basket around his neck filled with rose petals…."

Gary was still grinning. Sam knew the feeling. He'd had a smile on his face since they'd woken up that morning in his parents' house. Mom had insisted they spend the night before the wedding with them. It had certainly curtailed any… activity they might have wanted to engage in.

That was probably her plan. Mom is sneaky.

A knock at the door was followed by the sight of Curtis poking his head around it. "Are you two ready? All the guests are here." He gave Gary a look. "*All* the guests."

"Hey, best man, you sure you have the rings?" Sam fired at him. Through the open doorway came the strains of violins.

Curtis guffawed. "Will you quit worrying? This will be the smoothest-running wedding ever. Moira wouldn't have it any other way." He patted his breast pocket. "And yes, I have the rings. Five minutes, guys." He promptly disappeared back behind the door, which closed softly.

Gary put his arms around Sam and pulled him close. "Why, Senator, you're nervous."

Sam gave a shaky laugh. "Yeah, go figure. I can stand up in front of hundreds of people and quite happily give a speech, but the prospect of walking out there to where our families, friends, coworkers, and, of course, however many members of the press who decided to accept the invitation, is proving a little daunting." He peered through the window at the glorious late-April sunshine. "Thank God the weather is on our side."

"Since Barry Donovan declined his invitation, everyone out there is on our side too," Gary murmured.

"Yes, all two hundred and fifty of them," Sam muttered. "At least Hartsell isn't one of them."

Gary snorted. "He wasn't invited. And as a matter of fact, he's been awfully quiet since he didn't get elected."

"Give him time to get his breath back and I'm sure he'll try again in two years' time."

"And in the meantime, you can celebrate your landslide win." Gary snickered. "Pity Hartsell didn't do so well."

Sam cupped his chin. "I think we can afford to be magnanimous, don't you? After all, if it hadn't been for him, we wouldn't be about to get married." He kissed Gary slowly on the lips, and Gary melted in his arms. When they parted, Sam caressed his cheek. "Okay, that helped get my nerves under control. I think I'm ready. And besides, Curtis is right. This wedding is going to run like a well-oiled machine. Just as long as Becky and Josh haven't planned any more surprises."

The strippers they'd organized for the stag night still lingered in his memory.

Sam released Gary and walked over to the door. The music grew louder. "Ready?" he asked. To his surprise, Gary hung back. "What's wrong?"

Gary let out a sigh. "It was supposed to be a surprise, but we didn't know you'd be this nervous."

Sam froze. "*What* was supposed to be a surprise? And who, exactly, is 'we'?"

Gary bit his lip. "It was Curtis's idea, I swear."

"*What* was?" Sam was starting to panic. He could feel it bubbling up inside him. "Come on, you've gotten this far. Share."

"Well…." Gary sighed. "Maybe I'd better tell you. I wouldn't want you to walk out there and have a heart attack or something."

"Gary," Sam growled.

"There's… there's a special guest at our wedding. We didn't want to say anything in case it didn't work out, but apparently he's arrived."

"*Who* has arrived?" Sam's heartbeat raced.

Gary appeared to suffer from a coughing fit, from which only one word was audible. "…president."

Sam frowned. "President? The president of what?"

Gary swallowed hard. "The United States?" He looked at Sam from under those dark lashes, his chest rising and falling rapidly.

The world seemed to slow down. "You're telling me," Sam began carefully, "that the President of the United States of America is out there… at our wedding?"

Gary nodded and gave a weak smile. "Surprise!"

Sam stared at him in silence for a moment and then started laughing. "Did my mom know about this?"

Gary shook his head, a grin spreading across his face.

The shock began to dissipate. Sam chuckled. "This I have to see. This may be the first time in recorded history that my mom is speechless." He held out his hand and smiled at Gary. "Come on. Let's go get married."

Sam opened the door, and the two of them stepped outside into the sunshine.

Coming in October 2016

#19

A Matchless Man by Ariel Tachna

Lexington Lovers

Growing up poorer than poor didn't leave Navashen Bhattathiri many options for life outside of school. All of his concentration was on keeping his scholarships. Sixteen years later he's fulfilled his dream and become a doctor. Now he's returning home to Lexington and is ready to prove himself to the world. In doing so, he reconnects with Brent Carpenter—high school classmate, real estate agent, all-around great guy… and closet matchmaker.

Brent makes it his mission to help Navashen develop a social life and meet available, interesting men. Unfortunately Navashen's schedule is unpredictable, and few of those available, interesting men value his dedication like Brent does. Brent's unfailing friendship and support convince Navashen he's the one, but can he capture Brent's heart when the matchmaker is focused on finding Navashen another man?

#20

Suddenly Yours by Jacob Z. Flores

What happens in Vegas doesn't always stay in Vegas.

Cody Hayes is having one epic morning-after. The hangover following a Vegas bachelor party is nothing new to him, and neither is the naked man in his bed.

His apparent marriage is a different story.

Carefully plotting every detail of his life carried Julian Canales to a Senate seat as an openly gay man. A drunken night of Truth or Dare isn't like him… and neither is marrying a man he just met. He'd get an annulment, but the media has gotten wind of his hasty nuptials. If Julian's political career is going to survive, he has to stay married to a man who's his opposite in every way.Now he must convince Cody that all they need to do is survive a conservative political rival, a heartbroken ex, their painful pasts… and an attraction neither man can fight.

www.dreamspinnerpress.com

Now Available

#15

Stranded with Desire by Vivien Dean and Rick R. Reed

When their plane crashed, their desire took flight.

CEO Maine Braxton and his invaluable assistant, Colby, don't realize they share a deep secret: they're in love—with each other. That secret may have never come to light but for a terrifying plane crash in the Cascade Mountains that changes everything.

In a struggle for survival, the two men brave bears, storms, and a life-threatening flood to make it out of the wilderness alive. The proximity to death makes them realize the importance of love over propriety. Confessions emerge. Passions ignite. They escape the wilds renewed and openly in love.

When they return to civilization, though, forces are already plotting to snuff out their short-lived romance and ruin everything both have worked so hard to achieve.

#16

Marriage of Inconvenience by M.J. O'Shea

Lights, Camera, Lies.

Kerry Pickering has a problem. As a publicist for Hollywood bad boy Jericho Knox, it's Kerry's job to keep Jericho in the news. So far, Jericho's partying and public escapades have made it easy. But Jericho has a secret, and when that secret is revealed in the most spectacularly disastrous way, it's up to Kerry to spin it.

The team decides the best course of action is to make the public fall in love—with Jericho's secret committed relationship. The one that doesn't exist. Yet.

The team wants someone they can trust. Someone in the inner circle. That someone is Kerry. But what will happen when Kerry realizes that for him, the romance is no longer pretend? Can Jericho love him back, or is he just playing a role?

www.dreamspinnerpress.com